ODINSALL

The Stolen Children

By Cullen Spurr

© Cullen Spurr 2022

Dedication:

For Adam Hall, taken from us way too soon.

"Il est plus tard que vous ne croyez"

Table of contents

Chapter 1

RAGNAROK

"This is *BBC News*, our top stories today: Variant-19 death toll rises as thousands line the local hospitals. Tensions rise in the east as further sanctions are imposed. Fuel prices continue to soar as families struggle to keep the heating on this winter."

Val listened to the usual doom and gloom of the news as he sat silently in the passenger seat of his mum's car. His head was leant on the window and he watched the traffic moving at a crawl through tired eyes. This was part of his daily routine; the drive to school.

"Come on, you could have gone then!" his mum shouted as they approached the roundabout.

"Honestly, they must hand out licenses like Halloween sweets with the quality of some of these idiots". She complained.

She sighed heavily, shaking her head. She took a deep calming breath, just like her therapist had told her to and looked at her disinterested son.

"So, Val, are you looking forward to the school trip today?" She said.

"Not really" Val sighed. "I hate coach trips, don't I?"

He waved his hand laxly, still staring at the passing lampposts and leaning on the car window.

"Well, try to have fun whilst you're there. School life doesn't last forever you know, you're almost 16 so pretty soon you'll have to leave and get a job. Then you'll see what the world is really like". She lectured.

Val grumbled a wordless response. He continued staring out of the window, a glazed look in his green eyes, lamenting his coming coach journey.

Soon the car arrived, Val got out and his mum wished him a good day at school. He lifted his hand passively as he walked through the school gates and headed towards the dining hall to meet up with his friend Dan. Dan was a hulking boy with dark, tanned skin and brunette hair. He stood in stark contrast to Val who more closely resembled a beansprout, both in shape and complexion. Val saw Dan standing in the queue for cheese on toast and he walked over towards him.

"Ay up mate" Dan said gleefully in his standout Yorkshire accent. "You ready for this trip?"

"Morning" Val replied, yawning. "Not really, I hate coach trips."

"Cheer up you miserable git" Dan laughed, "No classes today, you should be happy!"

Dan punched Val in the shoulder playfully and Val smiled. The two queued together and Dan got his cheese on toast. They then walked towards class 11b and took their seats as the teacher took the register They, along with the rest of the class, followed the teacher out onto the front yard and entered the large white coach in single file. The trip would take about an hour and a half. Val took his preferred window seat near the back and Dan sat next to him.

"Hey" Dan said nudging Val, "what do you think of Kassandra?" He said gesturing towards the blonde girl sat near the front.

"I don't really know her" Val said.

He leant against the window with his head resting on the back of his hand, his preferred travel position.

"Mate. She's well fit, you don't have to know her, just look at her". Dan laughed.

"She's alright" Val said, trying to remain aloof.

However, Val agreed with Dan. Kassandra was beautiful: she was tall but not taller than Val, she had long legs, unblemished skin and big blue eyes you could get lost in. She was a bit of a know it all, she was always top of the class and on top of that she was the volleyball captain. If anything Val found her a bit intimidating, but that in itself was alluring. Not that Val would ever admit that to Dan, a slobbering oaf who spit out every thought that popped into his head.

"Alright?" Dan said incredulously. "Well who's better then, if not her?"

"Hah, wouldn't you like to know?" Val said teasingly.

The two continued in this way for the entire trip. Val barely even noticed the nausea he usually felt on coaches. The lumbering white giant passed a shaded sea of green farms and trees which decorated the sides of the winding country lanes. The rumbling coach rolled onwards and before Val even knew it they had arrived at their destination: York.

York is a medium sized, historical town surrounded by a large wall which was built by the ancient Romans. It has many historically significant landmarks, including the large Gothic Cathedral, York Minster, which was built in the 13th century and the Monk Bar gate houses which allow entrance into the town which straddles the river Ouse. Val hated that he knew all of this useless information about the town. That's history class for you, full of boring, unnecessary facts.

Some of York's streets are still cobbled, a fact that struck Val as very English. But the reason they were there today was for an educational visit to the Jorvik Viking Centre, a topic they were about to cover in History class.

"Right class here we are" the teacher said, "Line up and we'll get the tickets sorted out."

She fumbled around in her battered beige purse.

The class followed instructions and formed an orderly line. As soon as everyone was inside the teacher ushered them all onto the blue vehicles which moved through the Centre. This allowed tourists to see the recreations of the old Viking village that was found by York archaeologists some time ago at the '*Coppergate dig*'. Yet another fact Val now knew but didn't want to.

Val and Dan took the front seats of their blue vehicle as it began to judder through a dimly lit, recreation of a Nordic town.

"It's cool how realistic this is- but did they have to recreate the smell?" Dan said grimacing, his face twisted up dramatically as he held his nose and waved his hand in front of it.

"It is pretty ripe in here isn't it?" Val agreed, once again leaning his, now red marked, face on the back of his hand. His elbow resting on the side of the carriage supporting him.

"Shush" the teacher said from somewhere behind them.

Val jumped a bit, not realising she was so close, then settled back into his seat and zoned out to the narration of Viking life, drifting off to sleep almost.

Then came the screams.

A blood curdling, shrill scream that sounded like a woman, or lots of women.

Val jolted awake and opened his eyes but all he could see was black. He noticed that the smooth movement of the tracks seemed more turbulent than before, choppy even.

"Dan, did you hear that just now?" Val asked, only half noticing that Dan hadn't replied.

"Dan, you listening?" Val asked again. Once again there was no reply. What was Dan doing, was he asleep or something?

"Dan!" Val said irritably as he reached across to grab his friend.

Val clenched his fist and went to punch Dan in the shoulder as they always did to each other, but his fist didn't hit Dan, it carried on going as his arm stretched into the darkness, not making contact with anything. Val was sure Dan was right next to him. His face started to drain and he wondered where on earth his friend could have gone, but before he could say another word a blinding light lit up the path ahead.

The vehicle surged towards the light suddenly and Val had to hang onto the railing as not to fall out of his seat. He was scared and had no idea what was happening. If he could see them, he was sure his knuckles would be white as he held on as tightly as he could.

The vehicle surged forward, lunging towards the bright light which seemed to be enveloping the darkness that had surrounded Val. It was blinding, painful even, Val screwed up his eyes but couldn't bring himself to look away. Soon the white light was all Val could see. Then it came into view.

A spawling blue ocean amidst a backdrop of green mountains reaching towards the cloudless sky.

"Where am I?" Val wondered aloud.

Val looked around and saw that his blue vehicle was now a long, thin, wooden ship with round shields adorning the sides and a large mast in the middle boasting an even larger sail. Val looked to his right searching for Dan but he was nowhere to be seen. In fact, there was no one on the ship other than Val.

He was alone on a large lunging ship and he didn't know how to sail.

As Val's eyes began to adjust to the light he could just make out what appeared to be a large stone castle stretching out from the shoreline into the mountains. Strangely, this castle seemed to have a long wooden house positioned oddly in the middle of it. Like a long half oval that had been stretched out, and it was just sitting there, in the middle of this stone castle as if it belonged - standing out in such obvious contrast to the castle itself.

Val's vision adjusted a little more and he could make out a wooden dock jutting out into the water not far ahead of him. A figure that looked like a person was standing there, waiting. Was it even a person or was his eyes playing tricks on him? Val didn't know the answer but the ship continued steering itself towards the dock anyway.

After a few minutes it began pulling alongside the long wooden planks that made up the dock. Then the ship grinded to a sudden halt. Val stumbled forward, holding onto the railings for balance. He looked around but could not see the figure he thought he had seen only moments ago. Scared and confused, Val decided that his only real choice was to disembark. He gingerly got to his feet, struggling to stand up properly on the bobbing ship. He edged his way towards the dock and put his left foot onto it. This was a strange feeling as one foot was on solid ground and the other was still swaying. He bent down and used his hands for assistance and stood off of the ship and onto the wooden dock.

"Ah, you've arrived then?" A voice said.

Val jumped and nearly fell over. His heart was beating fast. He fought his body's urge to carry on facing the ground, dreading what he would see when he looked up. Trembling, he stood up to face the voice. Val looked up and was greeted by a tall, lean man wearing a brown fur cloak and boots and donning a menacing smile which chilled Val to the core. He was shocked and when he opened his mouth, the words just wouldn't come out.

"Come on then, follow me. I think you're the last one". The man said.

He turned towards the castle and waved his hand in the direction of the stone goliath, beckoning Val to follow him.

"C-come where." Val managed through chattering teeth. "Where am I?"

Then man turned his head and looked down at Val over his fur cladded shoulder.

"All in due time boy. The opening ceremony is about to begin. Now come." The man sneered.

He turned back to face the large stone castle and began walking towards it, taking long strides.

Val, having not the slightest idea what to do, decided to follow the man as he lead him towards the large castle, or more specifically the wooden oval house in the middle of the castle. It was only a short walk but Val's head was spinning to the point of eternity. He had to walk fast to keep pace, taking two steps for the long man's one.

Where am I? Who is this guy? How is this happening? All of these thoughts were swirling through Val's head as he trudged behind the tall man. He followed the man up a winding path and as he got closer to the castle he noticed two huge wooden, half oval doors. There was some kind of bird on each door, a black one on the left door proudly lifting its head to the left, and a gold bird on the right door looking slightly down and towards the right.

"What are those birds?" Val asked the man, slightly out of breath from the forced march.

"Those are All Father's ravens; Huginn and Muninn." The man replied without looking back at Val or even slowing his pace in acknowledgment of the boys loss of breath.

He then approached the ravens and whispered something. Val could have sworn he saw the left raven's eye move to look at the man but decided it was his own eyes playing tricks on him. The man stood back and with a loud creak the doors slowly began to open inwards and with a haughty push. Val was forced inside.

Chapter 2

WELCOME

Val was ushered through the large doors and found himself in a massive hall. There were tables lined with furs stretching half the length of the room with benches either side. On the tables were various meats and breads, enough to feed an army.

The walls were adorned with brightly coloured tapestries covering the bare wooden planks that formed the half oval shape of the hall. Throughout the hall there were bare smoke fires creating a warm atmosphere and an orange glow which bounced with shadow around the room.

At the head of the hall was a huge throne with a red velvet seat and golden arms and legs. Behind the throne, or possibly attached to the back of it, was a large golden spear with a fancily knotted rope attached to it, holding purple and green decorative feathers.

As Val was taking in the magnitude of this wonderous hall, he could not help but blink as tears formed in his eyes due to the sting from the smoke. Until now, he hadn't realised how cold he had been on the ship and he welcomed the warmth which the open fires provided. Shivering, he wrapped his arms around himself and realised his hoodie was damp. He was so frightened that he hadn't even noticed the sloshing water as the ship had sailed through the turbulence.

Despite the warmth of the room, Val noticed a cold uncertainty about the place as he realised that he was not alone with the tall man in this place. He looked around and the hall was crowded with others dressed in normal clothes who looked about his age and just as confused. Like him, many of them were shivering and holding themselves. Some of them stared blankly, wide eyed and still as statues. Others were rubbing their stinging eyes and looking around. Everyone looked scared, everyone was pale faced.

"Go join the crowd." The man said nudging Val more lightly this time, further into the hall.

"We will begin soon."

With that the tall man left through the large doors which swung shut behind him with a loud bang. Val moved towards the crowd of people, apprehensive, but in need of answers and happy to be away from the tall man. As he got closer he realised that no one was talking. There must have been over one hundred people in the room but it was utterly silent. Everyone seemed to be facing the floor and averting their eyes from him. No one was eating the delicious smelling food, not that he blamed them, and some looked to be crying.

"Who are these people and what's going on?" Val wondered as he edged closer towards them, still holding his shivering torso.

"Val?" Said an uncertain and distinctly female voice.

Val turned in the direction his name had been called from and stood before him, looking very uncertain, was a tall, blonde girl.

"Kassandra?" Val said, furrowing his brow.

"Val!" Kassandra yelled in a cheerful surprise.

She threw herself towards him forcing him to catch her. He unfastened his arms from his hoodie and reached out to prevent her fall. She was warm and soft to the touch. Val had barely spoken a word to the girl before now and he was a little taken aback as this acquaintance threw herself into his embrace.

"Val I'm so glad there's someone here I recognise. I was on that Jorvik cart thingy and then suddenly I was alone on a boat and a weird man dragged me in here." Kassandra said without stopping for a breath.

"It was the same for me!" Val exclaimed, happy that he wasn't alone in this strange ordeal.

"Do you know what's going here? Who are these people and where are we?" Val asked, now pushing her away and holding her shoulder. He caught himself in his actions and realised it was a little too familiar for a girl he barely knew. He released her and stuffed his hands deep into his pockets, tilting his head towards the ground.

"I have no idea. No one in here has said a word, you're the first person I've talked to and it feels like I've been in here for ages." Kassandra answered, ignoring his awkwardness.

Val considered asking some of the others if they knew what was going on, having a familiar face with him perked up his courage. But before he could turn around he heard a loud crack that made him jump, almost out of his skin.

He turned towards the noise and saw five people standing in front of the throne. There were four men and one woman, all dressed in furs and shiny armour. Shockingly each had a weapon and the man in the middle had a small black bandana covering one of his eyes like some kind of pirate.

The one eyed man took a step forward into the warm glow of the fire which danced on his battered face. The man had a wide white scare reaching down from where his bandana covered his eye. He had a long, white, braided beard held together with a gold broach and carved into it was a strange shape resembling the letter F. He had long and fancily braided white hair and more wrinkles than a prune. He was tall and thinly muscular wearing a hooded black cloak, lined with dark brown fur, which reached down to his feet.

"I am All Father." The man said in a quiet, but commanding voice as he opened his arms out towards the crowd.

"I am the one who has summoned you all here today. I understand that this is a trying and confusing time for you but listen well and I shall explain all."

By now the entire hall was looking at the self-proclaimed All Father, silently hanging on every word, either that or stunned into silence as Val most certainly was.

"Today, your world: Midgard experienced it's Ragnarok. Through fire and mushroom shaped smoke, as it was foretold so long ago. You are the last survivors of the Norse descended peoples, and some of only a handful of the remaining humans. It pains me to tell you, but your families and likely everyone you knew, who is not in this room, has perished." The All Father said solemnly, pausing as if to let the devastating news sink in.

Who just outright says that? Val thought scathingly. Even if it was true, you don't jus tell a room of school kids that their friends and family are all dead. When Val and his mother were given the news that his dad had died the police woman had sat them down and made them a cup of tea first. Granted, Val was pretty young when that happened and his memory was a bit hazy, but still, it's just common courtesy.

"What do you mean 'perished'?" A well-built boy near the front of the crowd shouted. He moved through the crowd towards All Father and his gang of armour clad men and woman.

"Do you think we're stupid? Kidnapping us and dressing up like the cast of *Game of Thrones* to scare us? Is this a new reality TV show or something?" He laughed uncertainly, turning to face the crowd and lifting his arms in an exaggerated shrug.

"I'm leaving, come on everyone." He said to the crowd, moving his hand in a wave as he began striding towards the doors.

At this a few of the others started to mutter in agreement, there was light chatting and the nodding of heads as members of the crowd also started to turn towards the door.

"Silence!" Boomed a large voice that cracked like lighting.

It came from the giant of a man stood to the left of All Father. Unlike All Father this man looked like a professional wrestler and had long golden hair and young, but hard looking face.

"You will not insult All Father in front of me boy!" The giant man shouted, swinging his overside arms and moving towards the boy who now looked, understandably, terrified.

"Stop Thor." Said All Father softly, sticking his arm across the giants chest to halt him.

"The young one's disbelief is understandable. It has been an age since the humans knew of our world after all. Perhaps a demonstration of your godly might will convince them of the sincerity of my words?" He chuckled, looking at the huge man through his one, small eye.

Thor smirked and pulled from his belt a large, decorated hammer inscribed with a strange writing similar to the F on All Father's beard broach. Thor lifted this hammer above his head and with a cocky look and a half smile on his face, he winked at the boy and suddenly lightning bolts flew out of the top of the hammer lighting up the hall with white and yellow.

Val looked up, stunned and amazed by what he was seeing. The entire top half of the hall was a lightning storm. Yellow and white jagged lines danced across the roof of the hall, cracking and booming as they went. It was like the most amazing fireworks display, easily out matching the New Year's Eve show in London – which Val and his mum watched every year on TV.

Val was amazed, shocked and terrified all at the same time and this mix of strong emotions made him freeze to the spot, unable to speak, unable to even take a single, scared step backwards. He felt something grab him and looked to his right to see an equally scared and entranced Kassandra, looking at the sky with eyes wide.

She peered at the light show from behind his arm, pressing her rosy cheek into him. He looked down and saw his hand clenched in hers. It occurred to him that It would have been a magical moment if not for the circumstances.

Thor dramatically raised his meaty hand and clicked his fingers. As suddenly as the lightning bolts shot out of the hammer, they returned to it as if they were being sucked in by a vacuum. He then took a step back, positioning himself back behind All Father. He now looked calmer and slightly more composed.

All Father took a deep breath and opened his mouth, signalling that he was about to continue addressing the crowd.

"Thank you Thor. Perhaps that display was sufficient to convince you of my sincerity young man?" He said softly to the boy who had made a fuss earlier.

The boy stood with his arms trapped to his sides, his face devoid of all colour and his eyes wide. He looked up at the one eyed man and nodded silently.

"In that case, let me explain to you all why I have summoned you here and what will happen now." All Father began, clutching his hands together behind his back and pacing in front of his armoured entourage.

"Many, many moons ago when Midgard was still but a sapling. My family and I visited your world and sired heirs with the humans. You may know them as Vikings. Over the years our offspring mated with normal humans, diluting their children's blood until most of your kind didn't have a drop of us left in them. You, are the exception." He said boldly, stopping mid pace and looking over the top of the crowd.

"When Ragnarok began in your world, with the introduction of a disease a few years ago, I began making preparations to save all that I could Unfortunately my powers, though vast, are not limitless and so I chose to save those most closely related to myself and the others you see standing before you. All of you are the direct descendants of us, the Gods, and I have saved you from death to allow you to be trained in our ways at this here Odinsall." He paused, the crowed transfixed by his words.

Val wondered if he expected them to thank him. The way he was going on you'd think he thought he was something special.

"Now I am sure you have many questions young ones and as such I will grant you three. You may begin." He said succinctly, stepping backwards and sitting down on the large velvet throne. He crossed his right leg over his left casually and leant back in his seat with his grizzled hands cupping the golden arms of the throne.

Val looked around to see eyes full of despair and confusion. No one seemed to be able to ask the question that Val believed was on everyone's mind, it was definitely on his. He hated public speaking and in school he'd always avoided asking questions in class, but this was different. With Kassandra still clutching his hand and hiding behind his arm, Val spoke.

"What about our parents? If we're your descendants, then they are too. So where are they?" Val asked, raising his one free hand outwards.

Some of the rest of the group nodded, waiting for the answer with baited breath and fearing the worst. They stared at Val and suddenly he wished he hadn't bothered speaking up.

"I only had the capacity to save one hundred and fifty of you and I made the difficult decision to prioritise the young adults. Babies and young children could not have survived the trip and the adults may not have survived the emotional trauma of being chosen over their children. This was the best outcome. I am sorry." The All Father replied matter-of-factly, tacking on the insincere apology to the end of his explanation.

There was a morbid air about the hall. Some of the crowd were crying and Val stood there, still and stunned. He didn't believe the one eyed man before when he said everyone he knew was dead, why would he? It was such an outlandish claim. However, after the lightning show, it was starting to sink in that maybe it was all true. After all, how else could you explain what had just happened to him?

His world had been shattered, turned upside down by a weird man in a bandana. He didn't know what to do with himself and became hyperaware of his hands for absolutely no reason. He could feel the trembling warmth of Kassandra's hand, clutching his. He was dazed and unsure if he even believed this All Father. Either way though, he didn't know where he was or how to get home and these 'Gods' seemed dangerous.

All Father had confirmed what he had suspected from the moment he set foot in the hall. He was alone, kidnapped, he had no idea where he was and he was beginning to believe that maybe his mum was gone. It was a dreadful feeling. Like nothingness enveloping his body and washing over his mind and if he wasn't careful he could drift into it, a drowning sailor unable to return to shore. Looking to his right he saw Kassandra now had her head lowered, he felt her puffy lips pressed into his arm and though he could not see her face, he could feel the warm damp of her tears on his hoodie sleeve. She was understandably mortified.

"Will we get powers like that lightning hammer thing then?" The loud boy from earlier said eagerly. There wasn't even a twinge of sadness in his tone.

Val was a little offset by the lack of emotion in the boy. He decided that he probably just didn't believe what All Father was saying. He was obviously treating this whole escapade like a joke. Val thought he'd recovered quickly from the white, still mess he'd become after Thor showed them his lightning hammer.

"You are one hundred years too young to handle power like this" Thor laughed light-heartedly, placing his huge ham fists on his hips. His entire body shook when he laughed and you could feel the bass of it shaking the hall.

"In time, perhaps some of you will develop powers akin to our own, but it is yet to be seen." All Father answered flatly.

"You have one question left, use it wisely." He said leaning forward and tucking his hands under his chin, his preened beard curling loosely around his wrists.

"Can we eat this food, I'm so hungry I can barely stand" A small, round boy said, eyeing the turkey legs on one of the long tables, his lips wet with drool.

At this the tension began to fade, more than a few of the kidnapped teens cracked smiles through glistening eyes and a few people chuckled. Sadness still clung to the air but it was a more manageable melancholy.

"Of course!" Said All Father, raising both of his hands in the air as he stood up from his throne. He cracked a smile and gestured towards the long, full tables.

"Eat your fill and we will discuss your sleeping arrangements when you are done." He said as the man to his right handed him a large tankard. He tipped it up towards the sky and wrapped his thin lips around it as his Adam's apple bobbed up and down in his throat.

He set the tankard down on the arm of the throne, wiped liquid from his furry mouth and clapped. More large tankards, made of some kind of animal horn, appeared at every seat up and down the long tables. People began sitting down and Val turned to Kassandra, trying to hide his pain with a smile, he said "shall we?"

The two of them sat down and began eating, not talking much as they did. Val realised that he too was famished and started piling his plate with food, as did the others. There was roasted turkey on the bone, chicken on the bone, beef, lamb, venison, pork, you guessed it, all on the bone. Accompanying the meat selection was different types of bread and fish. Notably there wasn't any vegetables in sight but Val didn't mind. If anything it was a nice change from his mum's health conscious salads.

"What drink is this?" Kassandra asked Val, holding out a tankard towards him.

Val grabbed the tankard and looked inside. He saw a thick amber liquid that looked almost like watered down honey. He took a sip. It was sweet but also had a kick to it, it burned the back of his throat. He turned his head and coughed, spluttering the floor with the drink and his phlegm. Wiping his mouth on his sleeve, he looked over at Kassandra, tears glistening his eyes from the convulsion.

"That'll put some hair on your chest." Laughed a voice from behind him.

Val turned to see the tall man who greeted him at the dock. His demeanour had completely changed, he was so serious before but now seemed almost happy.

"That's honey mead that is, it's the weakest drink we have, other than water, but it'll still get you if you're not used to it." He laughed and walked away to talk to some of the others at the table behind.

Kassandra and Val looked at each other and almost at the same time they burst out laughing. This continued way longer than it should have and

Kassandra had to wipe away tears of her own from the stomach-aching giggling.

"Well, after today's news I could do with a drink." Kassandra said as she tipped her head back took a big gulp from the tankard.

The feast carried on in this manner for a while until Val felt rather tired and Kassandra seemed a little drunk. His eyelids were getting heavy and he had to resist the urge to rest his head on the table. It had been quite a long day. Kassandra looked at him through half closed, dilated eyes. She way swaying ever so slightly even though she was sat down. It was strange how Val felt as if he had known Kassandra for his whole life, even though today was the first time they had really spoken.

Sharing a traumatic experience sure brings people closer he thought to himself and smiled contently.

He felt a guilty pang in his chest as he suddenly wondered about his best friend Dan. Since he wasn't in this room that must mean he's gone Val thought to himself, feeling guilty for enjoying himself with a girl whom Dan had commented on earlier that day. Val wondered, if Dan was here, if he would see it as betrayal. He felt sad again, it was a strange and emotionally draining day.

"Everyone, the feast is now over." All Father said, suddenly appearing in front of the throne again. He clapped his hands together once and the food and drink vanished from the tables.

"I hope you have all had your fill and that the mead has settled your nerves a little. However I am sure that you are all tired after such a long day." He began pacing again, letting his single eye glide over them.

"As such It is time to sort your lineage and place you into your clans so that we may assign sleeping arrangements." He said with an air of authority, still pacing like a general giving orders to his soldiers.

All Father paused for a moment, seemingly on purpose to build suspense. He stopped in front of the throne, turned to face the room and then clicked his fingers and two large ravens flew down from above carrying a large stone tablet. The ravens placed the tablet in front of All Father and Val could see some strange writing and a weird symbol on the stone.

"Thank you Huginn, Muninn." All Father said gently, petting both ravens on their heads in sync.

"Now, I will call each of your names in turn and you will step forward to have your blood deciphered and your clan confirmed." He said, placing his grizzled hands lightly on top of the stone tablet in front of him.

Val and Kassandra shared a worried look. What was the weird stone going to do? Kassandra squeezed Val's hand and he could feel a slight tremor in her.

There was a long pause whilst All father surveyed the room. As his eye passed over you, it felt like he was peering directly into your soul. It was a chilling sensation. He raised his hand coughed into it, clearing his throat. He gazed out at the crowed once more and said:

"Val Jones, please step forward. You're first on my list."

Chapter 3

THE BLOOD STONE

Val's heart leaped into his throat. Looking at Kassandra in disbelief as she stared back at him with those big eyes. Val took a breath and stood up from the table. He felt himself going red as the entire room turned towards him in anticipation. He hated being the centre of attention.

Val began walking towards the throne and, though it was in a hurried pace, it felt to him as if he was moving in slow motion. He passed the rows of people still sat at their tables, the weight of his steps feeling like a death march. His palms felt clammy as he clenched his fists, causing his knuckles to turn white. Finally he reached the end of the table and found himself standing in front of All Father and the stone.

All Father pierced him with his one eye's gaze, looking Val up and down as if picking out a prize pig for slaughter. Val let loose a single uncontrollable shiver, like a Mexican wave starting in his toes and ending as his neck snapped his head back. If he was stronger he might have given himself whiplash.

Now that he was closer to it he could see that the strange symbol in the middle was three overlapping ovals forming an almost triangle shape and enveloped with a central circle. Strange letters that were almost, but not quite, the same as the English alphabet formed a further three circles around the symbol.

"Ah Val, thank you for making haste at my call." All Father smiled, still sizing up the beanstalk standing in front of him.

"Now I shall explain how this ritual works. You will put your hand on the centre of the trinity knot." He gestured to the overlapping triangles in the middle of the stone tablet.

"And the seidr, or I believe it is called magic in your tongue, will decipher your blood lineage and determine which clan you belong to." All Father explained, looking at Val as if this all made perfect sense and that rubbing a weird stone in front of a crowd was a completely normal thing to do.

Val was overwhelmed. He had so many questions. His mind was racing, his mouth was dry and his throat felt like it had tiny daggers sticking into it from the inside. Mustering up all of his courage he managed to speak.

"S-sir?" Val asked sheepishly, his throat catching and his voice barely more than a hoarse whisper.

"What are clans and how does my blood have anything to do with them?" He asked, trembling.

"How forgetful of me. I have not yet explained this crucial step in your induction have I?" All Father smiled, tipping back his head and laughing as if this was all a silly bit of old-age forgetfulness.

"As I mentioned before each of you is descended from one of us, the five Gods you see standing before you. As such, the blood stone will tell us which God you share the most similarities to and that will be your clan." He began pacing again and Val struggled to follow him with his eyes and was forced to turn his head, like a metronome.

"I should probably introduce them as well shouldn't I" He chuckled, gesturing to the four people stood behind him and trying to calm the children he had just abducted.

"Well, as you know I am All Father and I am in charge of Odinsall. I will not have a clan, so those of you baring similarities to myself will be placed into the clan you share the second most similarities to."

"You have already met Thor." He said matter-of-factly, waving his hand loosely towards the towering blond giant with the zappy lightning hammer.

"He is the God of thunder and those who align with his clan are likely to excel in battle and will have the most potential for raw strength and fighting prowess."

"This is Bragi." The All Father said gesturing to a rather normal looking man with a pleasant face and short brown hair with completely shaved sides and a black swirly tattoo on the side of his head.

"Those who align with Bragi will possess the most potential for music and the arts. Gone are the days where battle was the only measure of a person's worth in Norse society. As you humans have grown in culture over time, so too have we Gods developed a fondness for culture."

Val found this a little hard to believe considering the weapons they all carried, their nonchalance at kidnapping teenagers and the lack of fruit and vegetables at the dinner table.

"This is Freya." The All Father said gesturing to the only female among them. She was stunningly beautiful with luscious blonde hair that covered her bosom, which in itself was eye catching. She wore sleeveless leather armour that dipped in the middle of her chest, and a short armoured skirt which showed off her long, toned legs. She wore large brown leather boots with for straps fastened into buckles, running up the sides. Her face was soft looking, with well-trimmed eyebrows and perky, hearts-bow, red lips. She reminded Val a bit of Kassandra, but more mature looking.

"Freya, as I'm sure is no surprise, is the God of beauty and hunting. Those of you who align with her clan will likely be blessed with good looks and the brains to match, you may possess skill with a bow and a fondness for cats."

Val thought that was a strange combination and began picturing Amazonian warrior women riding overside house cats through the jungle.

"Finally, this is Loki." All Father said, just slightly less warmly than he did when introducing the others. He gestured to a tall and slender man with incredibly pale skin and facial features resembling a snake. He had slit-like, dark eyes and bore an expression that suggested he'd rather be anywhere else but here. A sentiment Val and Loki shared. He was the only one, other than All Father, to wear long sleeved armour and a cloak. However, whereas All Father's cloak was brown fur-lined, Loki's was more of a shimmering green velvet.

"Those who align with Loki's clan will possess wit and cunning over raw ability. As he is the trickster God, you may also possess a certain flare for the mischievous." All Father sighed, looking over at Loki and shaking his head. Loki didn't show a flicker of acknowledgment and kept looking straight ahead, over the top of the crowd as if he didn't even know they were there.

"Now, whilst you are at Odinsall, your clan will be your family. You will compete with the other clans throughout your training and those who commit the most glorious deeds will be amply awarded. The clan who earns the most glory at the end of the year will have their names etched into this hall for eternity, and they'll receive a special reward as well. But enough of that for now." He finally stopped pacing and returned to standing behind the large stone. Val placed his hand on the back of his neck as it had gone a little stiff from all the turning he had to do to watch All Father's introductory explanation.

"Val if you would, place your hand on the trinity knot and we can get the deciphering ceremony underway." He said, holding his hand out flat with his fingers pointing to the intersecting triangles in the middle of the stone.

Hesitantly, Val reached out his left hand and placed his palm flat on the symbol. Suddenly everything went black, he felt cold as if he was falling through the darkness. His head was spinning and he could hear his blood rushing through his veins. He felt sick and if it was possible for him to fall to the ground he would have been helpless but to do so. He landed, softly and the spinning stopped. He was shrouded in darkness and a mysterious voice whispered to him.

"You know not the spirit of battle." The voice hissed, serpent-like. "Nor do you possess a particular beauty. You have no artistic muse and yet you are too honest to be a schemer."

"Where do I place one such as you, a son of the God of Gods with an equal lack of resemblance to his children?" The voice pondered.

Val attempted to answer but when he opened his mouth no sound would escape his lips. All he could think was that he didn't want anything to do with Loki. He was the most frightening of them all. Yes, Thor shouted and shot lightning bolts but he also laughed and seemed kind of cheerful. Loki however, wouldn't even look at them and All Father didn't seem overly impressed with the trickster God in his speech.

He shouted in his mind not to be sent to the serpentine man, send him to the pretty lady or the guy with the weird tattoo. They seemed more approachable. Just the look of Loki made him feel cold and uneasy and he trusted his gut.

"Hmmm." The voice continued. "It seems the fates shine unfavourably on you. An unwanted gift you share with only one of the Gods. My choice is made."

And with that Val could see again, he was stood in front of the blood stone and could see All Father still smiling at him as if no time had passed at all. One of the ravens lifted its wings, showing off its impressive wingspan. It raised its head to the side, like a painting and parted it's black beak. Val stepped back and lost his footing falling to the ground as the raven cawed "Loki clan" before returning to its previous, statuesque position.

"Interesting." Said All Father, but he sounded more disappointed than interested.

"Val, stand over near Loki if you please and I shall call the next person to the stone." He sighed and waved a lacklustre hand towards the uninterested, green cloaked man.

Val got to his feet and with his head hanging and his wishes unheard, he dragged his feet over to Loki and stood in front of him. Without a moment to waste All Father called the next name.

"Erik Erikson, please step forward." All Father requested, scanning the room with his eye once again.

The loud boy from earlier stood up from the far table and stepped forward, much more confidently than Val did. He approached the stone and without any guidance from All Father he placed his hand on the symbol. Immediately the raven reared its head and spread its wings and cawed "Thor clan" before once again returning to its statuesque pose.

Erik shot Val a superior look as he strutted towards the muscle bound God of thunder who had, not so long ago, shouted at Erik for interrupting. Val didn't even know this guy, why was he throwing shade? Earlier he was acting like it was us and them and now Val got the distinct impression that he fell into the 'them' category.

One by one All Father called names and the corresponding people stepped forward to have their bloods deciphered and their clans chosen. Slowly the balance of the room began to shift and most of the crowd was on their feet stood with their respective God. The clans were relatively even in members and as more people began to join Loki clan, Val noticed that some of the members looked older than he was.

The ceremony continued until there was barely anyone sat at the table. Val had lost interest at this point and found himself gazing at Kassandra. Her eyes were puffy and red, probably from all the crying she did earlier. She was looking around the room helplessly.

"Kassandra Johnson, please step forward." All Father said.

Kassandra gingerly got to her feet and holding both of her hands in front of her, as if stood respectfully at a funeral, she made her way towards the stone. Val looked on with anticipation and butterflies in his stomach. He wanted more than anything for his only friend and familiar face in Odinsall to be sent to his clan. Val crossed his fingers and mouthed good luck at Kassandra who was so adsorbed in the task before her that his wishes to her went unnoticed.

She approached the stone and at All Father's instruction Kassandra placed her hand delicately on the trinity knot, moving her head to face away from it. She scrunched up her eyes as if she expected it to hurt and the raven lifted its head once more.

Please be Loki clan Val thought as he tried to clear the thought of being alone again from his mind.

"Freya clan! the raven cawed and with a saddened glance towards Val, Kassandra left towards her new clan and was swallowed into its all-female crowd as they cheered, clearly getting into the whole school thing now. The Stockholm syndrome sure was setting in early, Val thought cynically to himself.

Val's heart sunk. It's strange how the splitting up of himself and a girl he had barely spoken to until earlier that day could be so painful for him. Yet painful it was. It stung and he physically felt his heart hurt. The perfect end to the most emotionally draining, terrifying day of his young life. Or so he thought.

All Father called the names of the remaining people who were subsequently sorted into their respective clans and then said:

"Ok, that's everyone aligned with their clan. If you will please follow your clan leaders to your new living quarters, you can then get a good night's rest. Classes will begin tomorrow!" All Father said joyfully.

He then snapped his fingers and he, the stone and the ravens all disappeared with a crack. The voices of the Gods started perking up requesting that their respective clans follow them. Val stole one last glance at Kassandra as the beautiful Freya lead her clan away.

He then looked towards Loki who uninterestedly beckoned to them to follow him. Loki walked quickly towards a wooden door to the right of the hall and pushed it open, Val and the others followed. He lead then through a winding path and up multiple staircases in a setting that had changed from warm wood to cold, hard stone. Val theorised that they must now be inside the large stone castle he saw from the ship.

After walking for what seemed like quite a while, Loki stopped outside a big, circular, green shield which donned the outline of a front facing wolf upon it. Loki placed his palm on the wolf's nose and the shield swung open revealing a circular hole in the wall.

Loki climbed in and Val and the others followed him hesitantly into a room filled with emerald green tapestries and chairs centred around a grand fireplace, much fancier than the fire pits in the hall. Once everyone had climbed through the hole the shield door closed and Loki finally spoke.

"Right then, this is your new quarters. The doors on the left are for the women and the ones on the right for the men. Each room is separated by age and those in your room will be your classmates starting tomorrow. Each bed has a timetable and uniform on it. Make sure you wear it and don't be late to class." Loki said in a rushed way with a bored sounding voice, his hands firmly clasped behind his back and his head raised, refusing to look at any of them. He then turned away from the crowd, his cloak billowing regally and he reopened the shield door, stepped out and was gone, leaving the door to swing closed behind him.

After a few moments of silence an older boy said; "I guess we should find our beds then" and with that everyone escaped their trance and fixed stares and started moving towards the doors. After a few wrong attempts Val found his bed along with four others, in the first room on the right. The youngest room, according to Loki's hastily given speech.

As Loki had promised on the bed was a timetable and a uniform. The uniform contained a pair of leather ankle boots, slim fit black rough-skin pants, an emerald green polo shirt with lace where the buttons should be and the same wolf insignia that was on the shield door embroidered onto the pocket. There was also a brown fur cloak with the same wolf again, embroidered onto the back.

The bed itself was a double bed with soft fur blankets and comfortable pillows. It was huge and luxurious compared to the old single bed and worn sheets he'd had back home.

There was a large window in between Val's bed and the one next to it, it was the only window in the room but it was too dark outside for Val to see anything. He also noticed that it had no curtains. Each bed also had an empty chest at the foot of it, presumably to store personal effects, though Val only had the clothes he was wearing when he arrived, and his phone.

My phone! He thought, I can't believe I forgot about it this whole time.

Val hurriedly pulled out his smart phone and tried calling his mum. However the long beeps of 'no signal' were all he heard on the other end of the line. He then tried to go on *Facebook* but that didn't work either. Even the *Google* search engine was inaccessible.

"Well I guess this is just a useless piece of plastic now." He said to himself half-heartedly dropping it into the open chest on top of the hoodie he had been wearing.

"Mine's the same." Said a timid sounding voice.

Val turned around and saw a smaller boy had entered the room. He had dark gingery hair and was covered in freckles. He was wearing a leather jacket and ripped skinny jeans and though he dressed like he was confident, his voice was very quiet.

"I'm Alex." Said the boy moving towards the bed next to Val.

"Looks like we're going to be in the same class."

"Yeah, I'm Val." He replied awkwardly, he wasn't always great at meeting new people.

"So, what are your thoughts on all this." Alex said quietly, turning away from Val and examining his new bed.

"Well to be honest I don't think it's quite sunk in yet. I'm still half convinced I'm going to wake up in my bed at home tomorrow." Val replied, only half serious.

"I know what you mean." Alex said, looking up from his bed furs and towards Val who was stood still with his hands in his pockets.

"It's been a rollercoaster of a day hasn't it? I just hope that things start to make more sense tomorrow."

"Yeah so do I." Val mumbled, looking at the floor and doing his best to avoid eye contact.

"So, who else is going to be in this room with us?" Val pondered. It was as much a wandering thought as it was a question for Alex. Val wasn't keen on the idea of sharing a room, especially if any of the boys looked at him like that Erik kid did earlier.

"I don't know, there's three more beds so I'm expecting some more. Where you from anyway?" Alex said, still quiet as a mouse but with actions that alluded to a more confident personality. He haphazardly tossed his leather jacket onto the bed and jumped on, placing his hands behind his head and his crossing his left leg over his bent right leg as if he owned the whole room.

"I'm from Leeds." Val replied, mimicking Alex and sitting on his bed, leaning backwards on his hands.

"How about you?"

"Sheffield." Alex said. He then picked up the timetable, leaving one hand behind his head. He gazed over it and then lazily tossed it as it careened towards the floor.

"Clan meeting with Loki first thing tomorrow. I'm sure that's going to be a barrel of laughs. That guy clearly wants to be here about as much as we do."

"I know, he's got this sinister aura about him too. I'm not a fan. Can't believe we got lumped with being in his reject clan." Val said spitefully. He wanted to be in Freya clan so he could be with Kassandra.

The two laughed and continued idle gossip. Val began feeling more comfortable around Alex which made it easier for his nerves when one by one the remaining three members of the room came in.

First there was Dean, a loud boy who seemed to enjoy making people laugh. He was brunette, with an angular chin and tree trunk legs. He played football at school before being transported to Odinsall.

Then there was Simon, he was a lot taller than the rest and even more of a beansprout than Val. He was a bit quieter and seemed to get on well with Dean. He was blond with a soft face and round, boyish cheeks.

Finally was Tom, he was short, brunette and quiet. The kind of guy who could fade unnoticed into the background. The one you would expect to see hugging the wall, alone, drink in hand, at a party whilst everyone around him danced and had fun. They might have that in common, Val supposed. Tom wasn't threatening or anything, like a stalker, but he definitely was not someone any girl would feel comfortable talking to alone.

That was Val's room, five average fifteen year old boys completely out of place, and their depth, in this strange new world.

After introductions Val went to lay down on his bed and as soon as his head hit the pillow he felt a tsunami of fatigue envelop him. His heavy eyes fell shut and he entered a dreamless sleep.

Chapter 4

CLASSES START

The next day Val awoke to the bright sun shining through the curtainless window. He sat up and moved to get a better look at his surroundings now it was light outside. He peered out and could see a row of small ships just like the one he had been brought here on. There were multiple wooden docks all situated on a large, clear blue lake. Behind the lake was an endless see of green hills and pine trees.

Val wandered back over to his bed and began getting dressed into his new, surprisingly comfortable, uniform.

"Morning." Alex said groggily, rubbing his eyes and propping himself up against the headboard.

"Morning." Val replied, one leg deep into pulling on his new trousers.

Alex got up and began to get dressed too, silently, for he was obviously not a morning person. Soon the other three of Val's roommates awoke and dressed and together they entered the common room where a group of girls were huddled in a circle by the fire. Some of the older boys were leaving their rooms at the same time.

According to the timetable, the clan meeting they had scheduled for first period would take place in the common area where they were now gathered. After a short while of conversation and anticipation the shield door opened and Loki entered. He walked towards the centre of the room, hands clasped firmly behind his back and his head held high. He gestured for the clan to sit down, which they did, some on the chairs and some on the floor. It felt like an informal primary school assembly.

"Morning, clan." Loki began, facing the fireplace and refusing to look at any of them.

"I'll try and make this quick. Basically, as per the old man's instructions we will have periodic clan meetings where I've been instructed to pass on news and check on your welfare." He sighed, obviously not thrilled at the prospect of having to babysit a bunch of kids.

"Since this is the first one I'll explain how your training is going to work. I don't like repeating myself so make sure you listen." He said, finally turning to face them. His eyes shot daggers at Dean who was making eyes at one of the girls and facing away from Loki.

"So, as I said last night you will be split into classes by age. As you may have noticed each door has a number on it, that number is your class's name and it's arranged in ascending order by age." He gestured to the number on Val's bedroom door, it said 'one'.

"Each of us clan leaders teach a subject which we specialise in but there are also other Gods and lesser Gods who will teach you other subjects such as history and writing in our language, as no doubt, you won't know how to." By now he was speaking through gritted teeth, intently staring at Dean who still wasn't listening.

"Your timetables tell you where to go and most classes will be mixed with one other clan's corresponding class. You will have tests and be involved in events throughout the year culminating in the final exams next July." A vein bulged from his forehead as he continued glaring at Dean.

"The old man's idea behind this school is to teach you all the basic skills you need to fit into our world and be able to be productive citizens, so make sure you study and give your all! Or something mushy and inspirational like that. Oh and call your teachers Sir or Ma'am, understood? A little respect goes a long way" Loki finished. Val was sure his last comment was passive aggressively aimed at Dean who hadn't listened to a single word he had said.

"Yes sir." The clan chimed back, like soldiers in a squad meeting.

"Sorry sir could you repeat that first bit." Dean pipped up, finally turning to face the clan leader.

"I was a little distracted." He said, winking at a pretty, and obviously older, brunette girl who, by the sour look on her face, did not appreciate the sentiment.

Loki strode nonchalantly towards a bookshelf in the corner, picked up a book as if to read it and without warning launched it at Dean. The book hit him hard in the face, knocking him out of the cross legged position and onto his back. The girls he had been staring at giggled at him. He did look a bit like a stuck turtle, Val thought.

Loki walked towards the shield door and said menacingly:

"The first thing I said was that I don't like repeating myself."

He began leaving the room and was half way through the round shield door when he stopped abruptly and without looking back at the clan, said:

"Oh, breakfast is being served in the hall. On days where we have no meeting you can eat there before classes. I suggest you hurry up if you want the good food because your living quarters are the furthest away from the hall."

He then left with a swish of his cloak and the shield door closed behind him.

"How's your face?" Alex said quietly to Dean, openly laughing at him.

"Shut up." He said indignantly as the clan started to leave the living quarters and make their way to the hall.

Dean had a large red line down the centre of his face stretching from his forehead to the tip of his nose.

His brow was furrowed and his, usually carefree, demeanour had gone. He looked positively infuriated. Val figured that he must not like being shown up in front of the fairer sex.

Val and his room followed after the rest of the clan, being careful to avoid the lip of the shield door. After a few wrong turns and at least a ten minute walk, Val and his clan arrived back in the hall from yesterday. Val noticed that there were now four, very segregated tables with table cloths of different colours. The only free table had an emerald green table cloth, so Val assumed that was their table, as it matched the colour of their new polo's, he sat down with the other clan members close behind.

Unlike the previous night Val wasn't very hungry and spent breakfast trying to catch a glimpse of Kassandra, to no avail. Meanwhile Alex was scarfing down food like it was going out of fashion. He was a fast and messy eater. He'd barely finish ripping off a chunk of bacon before gnashing at the bread or guzzling a glass of water. Val couldn't watch him, it was too off putting. There's nothing worse than the loud sound of chewing or seeing crushed food in an open mouth, Val thought to himself.

After a short time the gods started entering the hall and leading their clans away. Loki took Freya clan class one and Val thought he caught a glimpse of Kassandra's flowing blonde hair, but perhaps that was wishful thinking.

Freya sauntered over to the Loki clan table. It was like she walked in slow motion. Dean gripped the table and gawked open mouth. Her long, toned legs and short skirt made for an eye catching combo to a group of adolescent boys.

"Class one, follow me please." She said in an alluringly friendly voice. Her silky smooth hair swishing as she turned to leave.

Val and his four roommates stood and so did a group of five girls who must also be class one. The ten of them followed Freya out of the room and down the corridor to the left until they entered a warm, candle lit room with benches and tables lined in rows facing a blackboard.

"Please take your seats." Freya said warmly, leaning over a large, official looking desk at the front of the room.

Class one complied wordlessly, even the girls seemed to be entranced by her. Almost in unison they clambered over benches and obediently sat in silence.

"Now then, my name is Freya." Freya began. She stood up straight, making a slight arch with her lower back which nicely accented her bust. She held her hands behind her back, but unlike Loki, this act looked almost sweet and innocent.

"The class I am going to be teaching you is the art of seduction. By that I don't particularly mean seducing someone to sleep with you of course." She winked playfully.

"I mean using your charm and reading the other person in order to make them bend to your will and want to serve you." She slammed her hand on the table and the sweet, innocent teacher act shattered. She grinned at the class and Val realised that she had been playing a part to get a point across about her subject. It had worked, every male in the class had been transfixed by her.

"Seduction is an important lesson for you to learn if you want to survive in our world." She said picking up a long, thin pointing stick. She began lightly tapping it's end in the palm of her unclasped hand and pacing back and forth – like a captain briefing his troops on a war plan.

"Seduction is used in everything you do. From bartering, to leading a raid and of course most marriage contracts are created in the favour of the one who better seduces and charms the other." She giggled sadistically.

"So for today's lesson I'm going to get you out of your comfort zones. You're all young and inexperienced yes? So I want you to partner up with a member of the opposite sex and have a conversation. Practicing talking to those you may find intimidating or in an uncomfortable situation is the cornerstone of any seductress' technique after all." She said, halting her pacing, stepping forward and pointing her stick at them.

Val looked around and already everyone was moving towards a partner. He was going to be left alone. How could this happen? It was like playing football at school all over again and as usual he was being picked last. He looked around desperately and saw a girl, the only girl left unpartnered.

Val got up and walked towards the girl sitting down next to her and avoiding eye contact.

"H-hi." He said, nervously staring towards the blackboard.

"Do you want to be my partner?" He asked awkwardly.

"I think we're the only ones left." She said shyly and with a smile. She looked around and shrugged, Val caught the action out of the corner of his firmly averted eyes.

The girl was short and slender, as far as Val could tell under her uniform. Unlike his, the girl's uniform had a skirt and knee high socks as well as a polo shirt which seemed to lace down the chest further than the males' did. It wasn't so low as to be revealing, but just enough to make Val blush a little when he noticed. The girl had a delicate, porcelain face and wore her shiny, scarlet hair in pig tails.

Freya approached the two, holding her stick behind her back. She was smiling gently now, her attitude was closer to the innocent teacher than the squad captain now.

"Now, now young ones. I can hear your stammering from across the room. There's no need to be shy. Get chatting!" She said cheerfully, placing a hand on

Alice's back and pushing her towards Val. Alice blushed and tried to stop herself getting too close.

Val got a good impression from Freya, she was definitely a lot nicer than Loki. However, he also found her split personality a little scary, for obvious reasons.

"Kassandra is lucky to be in a clan with a leader like her." Val thought wistfully, remembering her tremble as she held his hand. Not that he was the cause of the tremble, but it was still the most physical contact he'd ever had with a girl.

"S-so, what's your name?" The girl said twiddling her fingers and trying to break the ice.

"My names is Alice."

"I'm Val." Val said, trying to look at her properly but still averting his eyes.

"Nice to meet you, where are you from?" He asked, doing his part to keep the conversation going, even if it was stiff elevator small talk.

"Nice to meet you too." Alice giggled, raising her hand to her small mouth.

"I'm from Harrogate, you?"

"Leeds." Val replied. He had noticed a difference in accent. She was much more well-spoken than he was, she sounded smart, something that definitely could not be said about Val.

The two continued like this for the rest of the lesson, gradually acting more normal and less like deer in headlights. Eventually Freya told them It was time for their next class and she lead them back through the door, down the hallway and down a flight of stairs. Finally, she knocked on a wooden door and left the class there.

The door was swung open and a beaming Bragi was stood there, gesturing as he said; "Come in, take your seats." Val couldn't help but stare at the swirly tattoo on the side of his head.

"I am Bragi." He said, moving towards the blackboard.

"My classes will cover our culture. From poems and flyting to skaldic verse and art, I will teach you all you need to know to understand our godly culture." He laughed. He seemed really different to the others, there was a light joy to him. His appearance said harden warrior but his friendly laugh said jolly art teacher.

Val looked around the room and could see a host of strange instruments. One looked like a large horn from an animal, there was also a small wooden guitar looking thing with a fat belly. There were various large parchments with paintings on them, though nothing like he had seen back in bis world.

Bragi then began to explain what flyting was. He told the students that it was a mixture of timed cadence and rhyme used to slander, brag, or retort to a foe.

Dean likened it to an old timey rap battle and earned himself a good laugh from the class.

Bragi didn't know what rap was but seemed happy that his students were engaging with him. Before Val knew it the class had ended, and no one had actually had a chance to try flyting since Bragi literally never stopped talking. Val had no idea how the guy was still standing. If a human talked that much they'd die of asphyxiation.

The day continued and Val and his class attended a history class where they had an introduction to the world of Gods and learned that it was the Gods who created humans and that they called the human world Midgard. They learned that there were nine realms contained within the world tree and they had simply left one and been taken to another. It was definitely closer to the lessons he slept through in high school back home, than Freya or Bragi's classes had been.

They then had to endure runes class which Val likened to torture. Learning to write again wasn't his idea of fun, he hated English back at his old school, but at least there he understood the alphabet. This was like being a little kid again. Alex shared Val's disgust at this and the two spent the entire class making faces at each other and pretending to shoot themselves with finger pistols when the teacher's back was turned.

Finally, after a very long morning, it was time for lunch. The weary class was escorted back to the hall where Val and Alex took their seats, this time accompanied by Alice who had started to take a bit of a liking to Val. This wasn't surprising as Val was the only person she had spoken to since arriving at Odinsall.

She nervously followed the two boys since Freya's seduction class. She hadn't really spoken to them and definitely didn't join in with the finger guns in rune class, but she was there. Val had noticed but his social skills were too poor to say anything, or to be overly welcoming to the girl. He supposed he didn't mind if she wanted to follow him, it was sweet and he wasn't used to female attention.

"I can't believe there are nine worlds." Alex said through gulps of chicken. "Do you think anyone has ever visited them all?"

"I don't know." Alice said, speaking to Alex for the first time ever.

"Didn't the teacher say that one of them is made entirely of ice and that giants live there? Why would anyone want to visit a place like that." She suddenly seemed much less shy. Val wondered if it was because the conversation was academic.

"Why indeed." Loki said sinisterly, appearing from behind them.

"Finish your food, your next class is with me."

Chapter 5

THE GOD OF BATTLE

Val and the others cautiously entered Loki's class room. Unlike the others they had been in so far, this one was dimly lit and had two parts to it. The first part was a normal classroom set up with a blackboard and benches. The other part was a strange training room with dummies and an obstacle course.

"Welcome to my class." Loki said, facing them this time and opening his arms.

"At the old man's request I am to teach you the art of deception. Listen well and do as I say and by the end of the year you will be well on your way to becoming a master of cunning and deception. These skills are needed to win battles when your opponent is stronger than you." Loki said proudly, scanning the classroom.

"And by the looks of you, most opponents will be." He sneered, is eyes lingering on Val's beansprout body for just a little too long.

"How would deceiving people help us to win battles sir?" Simon asked timidly, raising his hand as if he was back in high school.

"You'll stalk the shadows, use tricks and in some cases, you can even make your move on an unaware target if the opportunity arises." Loki replied, smiling menacingly.

"Sounds like *Assassins Creed*." Dean said mockingly.

Loki clicked his fingers and a large, hardback book appeared. Dean's eyes widened, shell shocked from his last encounter with a book. As before, he launched it at Dean hitting him squarely in the face and Dean fell off his chair to the amusement of his peers.

"You mean *Assassins Creed Valhalla*?" Alex laughed, for he had not seen what had just happened to Dean as he was busy examining the obstacle course from his seat at the end of the row. To his surprise no one laughed this time.

"You know, because they're Vikings?" Alex said turning around to face the class, just in time to see a second, larger book, soar through the air towards him. The book hit Alex squarely in the forehead and he too, was knocked off his seat.

Val stifled a laugh as a groaning Alex got back in his seat. He looked dazed and sported a familiar red line down the centre of his face. It appeared, Loki had deadly accuracy with a book.

"There will be no talking or foolishness in this classroom. Despite my reputation being that of the trickster God I do not appreciate children pratting about. Do I make myself clear." Loki said menacingly, slamming his fist onto the desk and glaring at the two boys he'd just hit.

"Yes sir." The class replied, a little scared.

Deception class went on and Loki spoke to the students about blending in to crowds and finished by saying that he would teach them his own brand of battle tactics later on as they were his clan, after all.

The class were then taken to Thor's classroom where the giant man waited for them next to the blackboard. He was so tall is head nearly touched the ceiling. Thor's classroom was set up like Loki's but with a boxing ring and weapons hung on the wall, in place of dummies and obstacle courses.

"Good afternoon young ones!" Thor boomed, clapping his meaty palms together.

"I am Thor and I am the God of thunder and of battle and since I can't teach you how to harness lightning, I'm going to teach you how to fight." He smiled enthusiastically, he seemed nice for an overside thunder giant.

Dean and Alex perked up at the word 'fight'. Val thought that Alex didn't seem the type, though he was a little bit excited as well despite having never even thrown a punch before.

"In our world we fight with both our fists and with weapons." He said, throwing and air punch and mimicking swinging a sword.

"As the year gets on I will teach you how to use weapons and we will have a raid battle. But for the time being, the All Father has Instructed me to start you off with hand to hand combat. He even made me construct this 'box-in-ring' as he thought it would be more familiar to you." Thor said, gesturing towards the boxing ring in the corner.

"Sir, it's a boxing ring." Tom said correcting him. This was the first thing Tom had said all day and Val was shocked that he, of all people, dared to correct the huge man.

"That's what I said." Thor replied, with child-like indignation.

"It's a ring because one fights in it, but it is square like a box. Box, in, ring." He said confidently, placing both hands on his hips, showing off his impressive biceps.

"No sir." Tom said. "It's Boxing, all one word. It's a sport where you fight with just your fists and you do it in that ring." Tom explained, standing and point towards the boxing ring in the corner. The class's heads moved between Tom and Thor, loving the drama.

"Oh, well either way. Tomorrow you are going to fight each other in it." Thor said sheepishly, dropping his arms and turning a little red in the face..

"Right, well, that's enough for today. Get to the hall for dinner and I'll see you first thing tomorrow." Thor said, obviously embarrassed and trying to hide it. Val noted that this was the shortest lesson he'd had and was certain Thor had ended early because Tom had upset him.

The class left as instructed and walked back to the hall together, chatting and laughing. A stark contrast from the atmosphere of yesterday.

"That Loki is a piece of work." Alex grumbled, rubbing his face.

"My head still hurts."

"Well you did make fun of his subject." Alice said, standing up straight with her head lifted high.

"There was no need for that though! If a teacher had done that back home they'd be arrested." Alex said pertinently, shooting her a sidewards glance.

"We're not in our world anymore though." Val reflected, walking between the two.

"We're going to have to get used to how things work around here. We don't exactly have a choice." He said glumly. The way Val saw it, there was no escape. He knew he couldn't survive the wilderness on his own, he definitely couldn't outrun or outfight the Gods and if All Father was being truthful, he was in another world entirely anyway. How was he supposed to get home? It's not like a portal back to Leeds was just lying around somewhere.

"Yeah I guess. I still don't like that bloody Loki though. He should be good to us since we're his clan." Alex complained, still rubbing his bruised face.

Val nodded in agreement as the three entered the empty hall and took their seats. Once again, dinner was a feast of various meats and poultry on the bone with fresh bread and handmade butter. There was also more honey mead. After a few tankards Alice became a lot more talkative.

"I wonder what the fights will be like tomorrow. Do any of you even know how to fight?" Alice said cheerfully, looking back and forth between Val and Alex.

"I've never really been in one." Val admitted, placing his hand on the back of his head and rubbing it slightly.

"I have." Piped up Dean, placing his hands on the table and half standing.

"There was this year eleven at my school who used to bully me and the lads and I socked him right in the jaw. Never bothered us again." Dean bragged, miming a right hook.

"That never happened and you know it." Alex laughed between mouthfuls of food.

"Alright, big man, how many fights have you been in." Dean retorted, folding his arms and sitting back down.

"One or two, nothing to write home about though." Alex said coyly, still more interested in his turkey leg.

"I've never even hit a punching bag, let alone a person." Simon said, looking down at the table and an empty plate in front of him..

"Same here." Tom agreed, eating a piece of bread and obviously not as bothered by his lack of experience as Simon was.

Val heard a familiar crack and turned to face the direction it came from. As expected All Father had arrived, this time taking his seat on the throne. He had his left hand resting on the arm of the throne with a bent fist against his face, keeping his head up. The skin around his eyes was dark and he looked tired.

"Good evening young ones." The All Father said to a now silent room.

"I hope you have enjoyed your first day here at Odinsall. Today your mentors have guided you around, but from tomorrow you will be expected to find your own way to and from classes. Some days you will be given free periods in which you can train down by the lake where the practice area has been set up, or you can study our world through the texts in the archive which is located in the main tower." He said calmly and unmoving, still resting his head on his fist.

"Now, before I bid you goodnight, I need to make it clear that this establishment has certain rules. Firstly, no students are permitted to leave their residence past the hours of darkness, you are also not allowed in the forest outside of lessons and you are not permitted to use or keep possession of real weapons outside of a training session. If any of these rules are broken you will be punished and you will bring shame upon your clan." He said firmly, gazing over the hall with his one eye.

"Well, that is all. Good night and may your studies be fruitful." He finished, more warmly.

With that there was another crack and the All Father was gone. The students began filtering out of the hall and returned to their bedrooms for the night. Val bade Alice goodnight as he retired to his bed large, soft.

Before going to sleep he looked out of his window into the darkness. He reflected on the events of the last two days and started to think that maybe this place wasn't so bad. He thought about his mum, realising he's barely said more than a grumble to her on that last car ride to school.

He sighed and was about to turn away when he saw a faint light heading towards the forest by the lake. As soon as he had seen it, it had disappeared. He did a double take but decided he must have imagined it and went to bed, conscious of the early start he had the next day.

The boys awoke to the sun shining through the window as they had the day before. They dressed and walked to the hall with Alice and the girls for breakfast. Val noticed that Alice didn't really talk to the girls, but they all talked to each other.

They were called Courtney, Alisha, Ellie and Beth and since none of them were ever away from their group of four, they may as well have been the same person to Val. They all kind of blended together. They were all brunette and had long hair, apart from Ellie who was blonde with long hair. They were all average height, meaning they were taller than Alice but smaller than Val. They were all relatively pale, though they looked like the types of girls who would have used fake tan back in their world. They all loved to gossip and whisper and giggle too each other. Oh, and none of them had said a word to Val so far, though they had all spoken to Dean – they probably didn't really get a say in that though, Val thought.

Val was hungrier this morning and managed some fried bread and bacon whilst Alex scoffed down a family of eggs, sausage, bacon and bread. Alex wasn't one for morning conversation and Val didn't really like to talk when he was eating. The pair were a match made in heaven. Alice on the other hand seemed to feel a bit awkward if no one was talking so she made idle chit chat and the two boys nodded or grunted back to her as they ate.

After breakfast was done they made their way to Thor's classroom. Upon entering they saw some unfamiliar faces in yellow polo shirts with a hammer symbol embroidered on the pocket.

"Ah, here you are Loki clan." Thor boomed, opening his arms and gesturing to the empty row of seats in front of him.

The Loki's followed his huge arms and took their seats at the front of the class.

"Today you will have class with my clan. I hope you're all ready for some brawling." He beamed, throwing a few air punches. He had clearly recovered from his embarrassment at the hands of Tom yesterday.

"I can't wait." Chimed a familiar, sinister voice.

Val looked in the direction of the voice and saw Erik smirking and looking straight at him. Erik was the loud boy from the opening ceremony. For some reason he still seemed to dislike Val, once again he was looking at him and saying challenging things – why me? Val wondered.

"Well then young Erik, that's the spirit!" Thor boomed, looking between the boy and the boxing ring in the corner.

"You can go first."

Thor gestured towards the ring and Erik compliantly stood up and walked towards it, taking his cloak off as he went and hanging it on the side of the ring. He ducked under the rope and stood in the far corner. He then started bouncing about and throwing air punches. He had obviously seen one too many fighting movies.

"Who will your opponent be?" Thor mused. He walked up and down the aisles, as if purposefully trying to create drama and stopped behind Val.

"Young Val, is it?" Thor asked, placing his meaty hand on Val's shoulder. It was heavier than Val expected.

"I think you will make a good first challenger. Up you get." He said, half lifting Val from the bench with that one large hand.

Val felt sick. His first fight was going to be against someone who was bigger and broader than him. To make things worse Val had a bad feeling about Erik. Something was definitely off about the way he kept staring at him, like he was calling him out.

Nevertheless Val compliantly ducked into the ring and, copying Erik, removed his cloak and hung it on the side. He didn't, however, start dancing around. He felt awkward enough just standing there, knowing the whole class were watching him. It made him feel queasy.

Thor stood at the side of the ring, holding onto the ropes and beaming an eager smile.

"You can fight however you like, but do not purposely break bones and if your opponent falls then back away and allow them to get back up. This is training after all." Thor said looking at each of them in turn.

Val moved into the corner and raised his hands up as he had seen in the movies. One fist slightly higher than the other, thumbs tucked on the outside of the first. Unfortunately that was as much as he knew.

"Begin." Thor boomed, clapping his hands together in lieu of ringing a bell.

Val moved out of the corner cautiously, after all, he had never even thrown a punch before. Erik moved towards him using one foot to step and drag the other behind him. He had done this before. Erik was leant forward and slightly hunched into his raised fists.

Val, not wanting to back down, moved forward and to the side until the two had met in the middle. Before Val knew what was happening Erik launched a lightning fast jab into Val's raised hands, testing him. Val was knocked slightly off balance and went to throw a punch of his own, his first ever punch in fact.

Val pulled his right hand back as if it was attached to a slingshot, but before he could throw the punch Erik jabbed him again, this time connecting with his jaw, and that was all she wrote.

Val's vision went black and with a loud thud he hit the deck. Erik had seen that Val's defence was lowered because of the punch he was trying to throw and had taken advantage of that opening. His jabs were lightning fast, maybe that's why he was in Thor clan.

Val opened his eyes, head spinning and realised he was staring at the ceiling. His head pounded like a drum and he couldn't remember hitting the floor so he must have blacked out for a moment. Great, knocked out without even throwing a punch of his own, in front of everyone. He started feeling sick again and it wasn't from the pain in his jaw.

"Erik wins." Thro boomed, jumping the rope and lifting Erik's arm in the air like a proud mum.

Val started to get to his feet and saw Alice and Alex, who had rushed to his side. At least they cared enough to check on him. It struck him as odd how close he felt to them considering how little time they had known each other.

"Are you alright mate?" Alex asked, ducking his head under Val's arm and helping him up..

"He'll be fine." Erik jeered, arm still raised.

"He's just a weakling. Didn't even get one hit on me did he? I guess that's what you'd expect from Loki's Losers." He laughed and a few members of Thor clan joined in, one or two repeating "Loki's losers" like a chant.

"Why don't you two take him to the healer to make sure he's alright?" Thor suggested, pointing in the general direction of the door.

"If you go back through the hall you can find her chamber off to the left."

"Ok sir." Alice said, ducking under Val's other arm.

Alice and Alex helped Val to his feet and the three of them walked, rather shakily to the healer's chamber. Alex was taking a lot of Val's weight for him, though he could have done it himself. Alice's attempt to help him was more of a token kindness.

"Are you ok Val." Alice asked kindly, looking up at him from under his arm.

"I'll be fine." Val replied, looking away and avoiding eye contact with her.

"What a piece of work he is." Alex said, quietly angry.

"Loki's losers? We'll show him."

The three walked through the empty hall and took a left as Thor instructed, arriving at the healers office. Alex knocked loudly and an old looking women answered.

"I've been expecting you, bring him in and we'll take a look." She smiled, moving to the side of the doorway and beckoning them inside.

Alice and Alex helped Val to a futon style bed on the floor, covered with furs. The old lady walked over mixing something in a glass. She was wearing a long, flowing, purple dress and had a bandana tied around her   head.

"Drink this." The healer said, handing the concoction to Val.

It smelled awful, but Val drank it anyway, and spit out some of it on instinct.

"It's not mead you know, just drink it and you'll be fine." The healer laughed, pulling out a cloth and dabbing his face where he'd spilled some of the mixture.

Val complied and drank the awful liquid and, to be fair, instantly felt a little better. His jaw still hurt but a least his head wasn't spinning anymore. The bitter taste of the formula stuck at the back of his throat though.

The healer seemed like a kind lady, though she wouldn't tell them her name, despite Alice pestering her about it. She insisted they just call her healer. It was an odd request, but, what wasn't strange about Odinsall?

The three stayed in the healer's chamber for a little while whilst Val regained his senses. Alex and Alice missed their turns to fight in the ring, but they were alright with that having seen what happened to Val.

Alex tried to cheer Val up telling him he'd beat Erik for him if they ever went toe to toe. From Alex's frame, it was probably an empty gesture, but Val was happy to have someone in his corner. Soon it was time for them to leave and they bade the healer goodbye, thanking her for her help and headed for their first sailing class.

Chapter 6

MIDNIGHT RENDEZVOUS

The three left the castle for the first time since arriving and met up with Dean, Tom and Simon on their way to the docks for their first sailing lesson. There was a warm breeze as the dew-laden grass danced along the path.

"Ay up Val." Dean chimed, slowing down to let Val and the others catch up.

"Took that KO like a champ didn't you?" He laughed, patting him on the shoulder.

"I won my match, told you I was a good fighter Alex." He said, proudly sticking out his chest and winking at the quiet boy.

"Give it a rest Dean." Tom sighed, his shoulders slumped and defeated.

The group laughed and arrived at the docks. They were sharing this class with Freya clan and Val was hopeful that he might see Kassandra again. Freya clan wore dark red polo's and had a cat symbol on their breast pockets. Val looked into the sea of red as he walked towards the dock but he couldn't find Kassandra anywhere.

"This lot are all girls." Dean observed, turning and pulling a face at the others..

"What I wouldn't give to be in that clan." Simon said, sounding like he was spending too much time with Dean.

Alice shook her head lightly, but didn't say anything.

Looking towards the lake, the group could see a large purple sail coming towards them. As it neared a figure could be made out standing at the front of the ship and holding a rope. The figure docked the ship, lowered the purple sail with one swift flick of his wrist and then came ashore.

"I am Njord." The man said, taking slow strides towards them.

He was stocky and small with a long brown beard and a head shaved at both sides with the top swept back into a long ponytail.

"I'm the God of sailing and it's my job to teach you young'uns how to navigate the great blue." He said with a slight country twang.

"Watch out or he'll steal your tra-err." Dean whispered, putting on his best impression of their new teacher.

"I heard he's got a brand new combine harvester and he'll give you the key." Simon whispered back and the two stifled a laugh.

"A big part of our culture revolves around sailing This here realm of the Gods is actually a collection of lots of islands and to go from place to place you need a boat and the know how to use it." Njord said, standing still with his hands in his pockets.

Njord continued by explaining the parts of the boat. The rudder for steering, the sail for propelling the boat forward using the wind and the oars for when there was no wind. They didn't actually do any sailing in their introductory lesson, much to Val's relief. Njord did, however, promise them a go in the little two man row boats next time.

All in all it was just a boring lecture. The only saving grace was that they got to be outside in the beaming sun.

When Njord had finished, they left and began heading back towards the castle for dinner. Alex was starving, or so he moaned multiple times in hushed whispers to Val throughout the lecture.

"Val!" Someone shouted from behind him.

Val turned around and saw Kassandra waving to him, her blonde hair blowing in the wind almost in slow motion. It reminded him of the big purple ship's sail, but much more majestic.

"I'll catch up with you guys later." Val said to his friends as he dropped back to let Kassandra catch up.

"Hey." Val said nervously, placing his hands into his pockets.

"Hey yourself." Kassandra said, grabbing Val's arm and putting her mouth next to his ear, sending a shiver throughout his entire body.

"Meet me down by the docks after lights out tonight ok?" She whispered.

Kassandra then bounced away towards a group of beautiful girls who made up the Freya clan.

One thing to note about Freya clan, other than it being a girl-only clan. They were also all blonde, none of them were small, they all had athletic bodies and not a single one of them was flat chested. They were all stunning, but it was also hard to tell them apart in a group.

Val walked into the hall a little dazed and sat down between Alex and Alice who had saved him a seat at the table.

"Who was she." Alex smirked, stopping eating to shoot Val an approving glance amid raised eyebrows.

"A girl from my old school back in our world." Val answered innocently, waving his hand as if it was nothing.

Val liked this kind of attention though. A pretty girl had spoken to him and his new friend had seen. Was he cool now? He wondered.

"Ooh, someone special?" Alex asked slyly, elbowing Val in the ribs.

"Actually I'd never even spoken to her until we got here. She was just in my class." Val replied coolly.

It wasn't a lie, but he also thought it made him sound better than he was. In actual fact Kassandra had only spoken to him cause she knew who he was and she was scared. It was a completely normal and understandable reaction. If it wasn't for these very odd circumstances she'd likely have never looked at him twice. But Alex didn't need to know that.

"If you say so." Alex teased, returning to his ham hock.

Alice didn't join in on this conversation and she seemed a little off to Val but he brushed that notion aside, ate and went back to the residence with the group.

A little while later as the boys were bedding down, Val was nervously looking around the room, waiting for his chance to sneak out. From his bed he gazed out of the window longingly, butterflies dancing in his stomach. There was a dim flicker of a light in the darkness, it seemed familiar to Val but he was too preoccupied to give it any real thought.

When it seemed like all of the boys were asleep, Val made his move. He tiptoed across the room and slipped through the bedroom door, taking care to hold the handle down as he closed it, to avoid noise.

He clambered out of the shield door and made his way down the dark corridor. Odinsall looked different at night, it was pitch black and so quiet that Val became aware of his own heart beat and breathing. It was an uncomfortable feeling.

Clinging to the walls for guidance he eventually found his way to the empty hall and from there, outside.

It was still dark outside but the natural light from the crystal clear stars above made it easier to navigate than in the castle. Val crept down to the docks where a dark figure awaited him.

"Val, is that you?" Kassandra whispered from in the darkness.

"it's me." Val replied, stumbling towards her outline, shadowed against the moonlight.

"Good, I'm glad you came. Come with me." Kassandra said, reaching out and grasping his hand.

Val dutifully followed Kassandra down to the edge of the banking that bordered the lake. He saw a small boat, one of the training boats that Njord had mentioned in class earlier that day. Kassandra gracefully stepped inside and took a seat. Val followed gingerly, the boat rocked as he put his weight on it and he was certain he was going to fall in – but he didn't.

"Do you think you can row us out a bit?" Kassandra asked in a hushed tone, looking at a pair of oars nestled in the boat.

Val wasn't certain that he could, he hated transport and he'd never rowed a boat in his life. However, he felt compelled to say yes and he took both oars in his hands. He let them slip into the water and pulled, lifting them out as he pushed them back and repeated the action. He'd seen it done before and was pretty sure he was getting it right.

It was much harder work than he expected. His back and arms felt like they were going to explode, but he was never going to let Kassandra know that. After a short while of rowing in silence Kassandra asked Val to stop.

"This should be far enough." Kassandra said from the darkness.

"How are you doing Val? I haven't seen you since we arrived."

"I'm getting used to things I think, some of the people in my clan are pretty cool. How about you?" Val replied, pulling the oars in and letting them slide down the side of the boat.

"The girls in my clan are a bit up themselves, but I think I like most of them. Though it does feel like I'm in an episode of *Gossip Girl*, just without the nice clothes and money." She giggled, lifting her shadowed hand to her mouth as she did.

Val had never seen *Gossip Girl* so he didn't really get the reference but he reciprocated the laugh anyway.

"Anyway Val." Kassandra began, sounding more serious now.

"I asked you out here because I never really got the chance to thank you before. I was so scared when it all happened and having you there as a familiar face really helped." She said sincerely, her big blue eyes looking at him from the dark.

"You know, you didn't have to bring me all the way out here to say that." Val laughed, scratching the back of his head.

"I know, but I wanted a private moment with you to say thanks. That's all." She said, hunching her shoulders and placing her hands between her legs.

"Anytime." Val smiled.

"Val, I'm trying to adjust but this place, it's still so new and different. I miss my mum and dad and I miss school and my friends." She said and then abruptly stopped, as if catching herself letting something slip.

"I'm sorry, I shouldn't have just blurted all of that out like that. It's just, I feel like I can be more honest with you since we kinda knew each other. Is that stupid?" She asked, pushing her hands further into the space between her closed legs.

"No, not at all." Val said empathetically.

"I, actually, feel the same way." He said quietly, as he started to play with his finger nails.

Kassandra moved closer to Val and wrapped her arms around his, silently sobbing and thinking of home. The two sat in silence for a while, looking at the stars and in that moment, for the first time since arriving here. Val felt truly peaceful.

He lifted his free arm and cautiously placed it on her head. He stroked her hair, it was soft and a little cold. He could feel her bare legs touching the tip of his fingers as she cuddled into the arm she'd claimed. His chest thudded hard and he hoped she couldn't hear it.

Kassandra lifted herself away from Val and sat back in her seat on the boat. She wiped her eyes on her sleeve and composed herself again.

"Shall we head back?" She said quietly, looking in the direction of the castle.

Val wordlessly took up the oars once again and rowed the two back to the shore. He jumped out of the boat, trying not to fall in the water, and offered Kassandra a hand. She took it politely despite being capable enough not to need his help.

They walked back towards the castle together.

"Thanks for tonight." Kassandra whispered, looking away from Val.

"We can do it again sometime if you want?" Val said hopefully, hands now back in his pockets.

"Maybe if you're lucky." Kassandra said playfully. She leaned in and as light as a fairy, she kissed him on the cheek. Then, as if by magic, she was gone and Val was alone in the dark in front of the castle.

It's a good job it's dark, Val thought, face flushed like a tomato as he headed back to his room and crawled into bed, smiling.

Chapter 7

MISSING STUDENT

The next morning Val and the others rose once again to the sunlight streaming in through the curtainless window and headed to breakfast. Val, still tired from the previous night's escapades, struggled to eat his breakfast.

"Where were you last night?" Alex said casually through a mouthful of bread.

"What do you mean?" Val replied sheepishly, chasing a sausage around his plate with a fork.

"I saw you leave and you woke me up coming back in." Alex laughed, tearing into a bacon medallion.

"I was with Kassandra." Val said quietly, hand on his face and staring at his uneaten food.

"Oh really? I should have guessed. Bit of other worldly shenanigans?" Alex teased, nudging Val with his elbow.

"N-no! Nothing like that." Val said flustered, finally looking up from his food.

"And since when do you say shenanigans? Is this world starting to rub off on you?" He laughed, giving Alex a look through furrowed brow.

"You snuck out last night!" Alice interjected, eavesdropping.

"You heard the All Father's rules. No leaving the residence after dark. You'll get the whole clan in trouble." She whisper-shouted pointing her soiled breakfast knife at Val.

"Since when do you care." Alex said through a mouthful of sausage.

"It's not like any of us want to be here, why should we care about winning some competition?" He asked, shrugging his shoulders at her as he continued eating.

"You might not want to be here, but like it or not, this school is run by Gods. Gods who saved us from dying. We can't go back home so we have to try and make the best of this world." She argued in hushed tones.

She was right of course. None of them could go home, it was the logical approach to just make the best of it. At the very least, it offered them the best chance of surviving this strange new world, or so Val thought.

Simon stood up from further down the table and walked towards Val and the others.

"Have any of you guys seen Tom?" Simon asked, looking up and down the table.

"No." Val replied, not particularly concerned.

"Is he not with you and Dean?" He asked casually flipping a piece of fried bread with his fork.

"Nope, we haven't seen him since last night and he wasn't in bed when we woke up this morning." Simon said, a glint of worry in his eyes.

"I'm sure he's around, we'll see him in class." Alex said, through yet another mouthful. His table manners were awful but his appetite was in a class of its own.

Breakfast drew to a close and Loki clan went to their first class of the day: seduction with Freya. Loki and Thor clans were sharing this class today and as Val walked in he could see Erik sat on the table, glaring at him as he walked in. Erik whispered something to a gaggle of Thor clan sat near him and they all began laughing and looking at Val.

"Just ignore them mate." Alex said as they took their seats on the other side of the room.

Freya walked in and took up her position at the front of the class. She scanned the room with a confused expression.

"Are you missing one Loki clan? There are normally ten of you." She asked, placing her hands on her hips, accenting the short armoured skirt she wore.

"It's Tom." Simon said from the back of the room.

"We haven't seen him today."

"Hmm, well I'm sure he's around somewhere. We'll begin without him." Freya said, turning to the blackboard and scribbling something in runes.

It was the same story all day. Tom wasn't in history class or runes class either and he didn't show up for dinner that evening. At this point Simon and Dean were really worried and even Alex had to admit something was wrong. In the residence later that night, whilst sat by the fire in the common area the group chatted.

"Something is definitely going on here." Dean said, stood in front of the fire facing solemnly away from the group.

"Yeah, how can he have been missing for a full day." Simon agreed, nodding from his arm chair.

"You don't suppose he's just left do you?" Val suggested. He was sat on the floor leaning back onto his elbows.

They were the only ones in the common area, it was already dark outside. The older students and the class one girls were already in bed.

"Left to go where?" Alex said, leaning against a wall.

"I don't know, maybe he went for a walk in the forest or got lost in the castle somewhere. I mean it's big enough." Val replied, trying to think of where Tom could have gone.

"Nah, he was way too much of a scaredy cat for that. I don't think he would have gone off on his own." Simon said, forcing a slight laugh.

"The real question is, how are we going to find him?" Dean said.

He was right. How were they going to find him? The castle was huge and the teachers didn't seem overly concerned. Back in their world a missing kid would be cause for the police to get involved, by now there'd probably be appeals on social media. Here, however, no one seemed to care.

"We're not." Alice said, appearing from the girl's room.

"We should tell one of the Gods and let them handle it. They probably have location magic or something anyway." She said, folding her arms.

"She might be right guys." Val agreed.

He'd already gotten on Alice's bad side once today by sneaking out the previous night. He wasn't keen to have more knives pointed at him.

"Well who do we tell then?" Dean said irritably, turning to face the group.

"Definitely not Loki." Alex growled.

"I get a bad feeling from him and he probably wouldn't even care." He tutted and shook his head.

"All Father would be the best one to tell." Simon said.

Val thought that was a solid idea. All Father was in charge here, he probably knew the castle and surrounding area better than anyone else.

"I agree." Alice said, moving towards the centre of the room.

"But the problem is how to contact him, he just appears and disappears."

"Do you think he has a chamber in the castle somewhere." Val asked.

"Probably, but the question is where?" Alice replied, lifting her hand to her chin.

Where would All Father's chamber be? The castle was huge but Val was pretty sure they'd seen most of it by now. He'd only ever seen All Father in the hall and he always just seemed to appear.

"Isn't there a huge tower behind the hall?" Alex said, removing his hands from his pockets and crossing them instead.

"You can see it from outside, like when we were doing sailing lessons the other day."

"Now that you mention it, I noticed that too." Simon said from his leather clad chair.

"But how do we get to it?"

"Maybe there's a secret entrance in the hall?" Dean said excitedly, moving away from the fireplace.

"Let's go have a look!"

"No you can't, it's dark outside we'd be breaking the rules." Alice complained.

"This is more important than rules." Dean said.

Val wondered if he might have an ulterior motive and just fancied a midnight sneak-out.

"Let's go!"

With that Dean was up and heading towards the shield door and the boys were hot on his heels. With a sigh, Alice reluctantly followed behind them. The group crept through the dark, winding corridors. They tried to tread quietly but every footstep, no matter how light, seemed to echo.

They were tense and a little on edge as the big, stone castle was cold and eerie at night. Eventually though, they made it to the hall unscathed and without being caught.

Once inside the hall the group split up, looking for an exit that they hadn't used before. They all knew about the large raven doors that lead outside and they knew about the two doors on the left and the right of the hall that lead to the residence and the classes. However, other than using these doors and sitting at the tables for meals, no one had actually looked around the hall properly before.

Dean headed over to the throne and took a seat.

"I am the ruler of the realm of the gods!" He laughed, covering one eye.

"Get off of that you idiot." Alice said, shaking her head.

"What if someone walks in and sees you, we'll be in so much trouble." She whisper-shouted from across the room.

"No need to worry, I'm the ruler of these Gods, they can't punish me." Dean said, sticking his thumb to his chest and raising his head.

Dean laughed at his own joke and leaned backwards in the throne which unexpectedly tilted.

A crunching sound echoed through the hall like a key turning in a lock and the throne slid backwards revealing a stone staircase leading underground.

"Well that's creepy." Val said, peering through the hole into darkness.

"Come on, let's go down. Someone must have heard that noise." Alex said heading down the passage.

The others followed and the entrance closed behind them trapping them inside. They walked down the stairs for what seemed like forever. It was pitch black and navigating the stairs without tripping wasn't easy. Eventually the floor levelled out and they continued walking. Alice tripped on a loose stone and grabbed Val's arm. He could feel her trembling and the two walked together behind the rest of the group.

After walking a short distance a light appeared ahead of them. They headed towards it, Alice shook the entire time, still clinging to Val's arm. They reached the source of the light and saw that it was actually a blue, electric field looking thing.

"What is that?" Simon asked, gazing up at the shining blue barrier.

"I don't know." Alex replied, reaching out his hand to touch it but pulling it away as he thought better of it.

The glow from the electric field bounced off the walls revealing a circular room with no other way In or out apart from the passage they had walked down.

"There's nowhere else to go. Maybe this light does something?" Alex said, still wrestling with the desire to touch the swirling blue glow.

Unable to control himself any longer, Alex stepped into the light and disappeared.

"Oh my god, where has he gone?" Alice said panicked, she gripped Val's arm harder, digging her nails into him. He winced a little and placed his hand on hers, hoping to calm her down and ease her claw like grip.

"Only one way to find out." Dean said gleefully.

Dean skipped into the light and vanished. Simon then followed suit, closing his eyes and stepping hesitantly into the blue glow.

"I think we should go too." Val said to Alice who was still clinging to his arm and trembling.

"Mhmm." Alice nodded unconvincingly.

The two walked into the light together and Val felt it's warm embrace. Alice shut her eyes tightly as they stepped in, gripping his arm hard.

"Open your eyes." Val said gently.

Alice reluctantly opened her eyes and realised she was now in a well-lit room. She looked around and saw a golden desk with ink pots and parchment. There was a bear skin rug on the floor and paintings of battle scenes and great landscapes on the walls. There was a roaring fireplace to the right and a wall full of books to the left. Alice noticed that some of these books were from her world.

Behind the golden desk was a large perch with the two ravens, Huginn and Muninn, sat atop it. One of them opened its lazy eyes and looked at the group before closing it and turning its back on them.

"Think this is it?" Val said, walking slowly towards the desk and looking around.

"It's got to be, who else keeps two ravens?" Dean said, sniggering.

"Who goes there!" A loud voice boomed.

The group collectively jumped and Alice began clutching Val's arm again. One of the large battle paintings swung open suddenly revealing a doorway and the All Father stepped through. He took a few strides and stood tall behind his golden desk, his one eye looking at each one of them in turn.

"Loki clan, class one." He said, placing his long arms on his hips.

"What compels you to break my rules and sneak into my chambers this eve?"

"W-well sir." Dean began, backing away slightly.

"We wanted to tell you that our friend Tom is missing. We haven't seen him all day."

"Ah, worried about your clansmen?" All Father smiled, dropping his stern expression and taking a seat behind his desk.

"A noble pursuit indeed." He nodded, placing his arms in front of him on the desk.

"We wanted to tell someone sir and you were the only one." Val said, moving from out of the shadows where he had been stood.

"Do not fret young ones. I am well aware of your missing friend." All Father said, placing his chin on his fists.

"This castle is vast and filled with secrets, much like the one you have stumbled upon in your quest to find me." He winked at Dean.

"I will find your friend, I am sure."

"Oh, you knew already?" Dean said, sounding surprised.

"Of course I did." All Father said.

"Now, I will not punish your rule breaking this once as it is a noble cause to try and help ones allies. But, if you break my rules again there will be punishment, regardless of the reason." He said gently.

"Now, I shall return you to your residence where you will get some sleep and leave the issue of young Tom in my more than capable hands. Understood?"

"Yes sir." The group said in unison.

"Oh and Dean." All Father said, shooting him a knowing and cheeky glance.

"Yes sir?" Dean gulped.

"Next time you want to impersonate me, try to be more creative than simply covering your eye with your hand." He said.

Dean flushed bright red. All Father clicked his fingers and the group were back in front of the fireplace in their residence.

"H-how did he know?" Dean asked quietly, looking at the hand he'd used to cover his eye on the throne.

The boys bade Alice goodnight and returned to their bedroom. Val began bedding down and stole one last look out of the window into the blackened night. Once again he saw a flicker of light near the forest, he blinked and it was gone. He then climbed into bed, under the heavy fur covers and fell into a deep, exhausted sleep.

Chapter 8

YULE

The weeks past and still there was no sign of Tom. More worryingly, Val had heard rumours that students had gone missing from the other clans as well. There was a tense air around the castle as students began travelling exclusively in groups. The Gods had tried to address this issue, brushing it under the rug, so to speak, in their respective clans. This, however, had done nothing to quell the growing worries and fears beginning to surface among the students who were still very much new to this world and it's ways.

Through the weeks Val and his class had spent more time in Loki's cunning and deception class. Thanks to Dean's joke in the introductory class, the students had taken to calling it the assassination class.

Val was a very average student, he wasn't terrible at most subjects but he also never stood out or showed any particular talent. He certainly wasn't gifted in anything really. However, despite a growing dislike of the sarcastic and often mean trickster God, Val was actually quite good at assassination class.

One day in particular, Loki had taken the class to the outdoor training area. He tried to teach them about using shadows and physical cover to hide yourself. The problem was, his lacklustre teaching style cruel beratement of students he deemed to be unworthy of his clan, which was all of them, didn't inspire much enthusiasm.

In one particular class they had been playing hide and seek and Val actually won. He never won anything. Maybe it was because he was so average that he was getting good at blending in, who knew? Either way he was taking to the art of physical deception quite well.

Erik, of course, lamented assassination class and took every opportunity to voice this opinion of his. To Erik, there was no honour in skulking in the shadows when you could face your opponent head on and throw punches. Val presumed this dislike for the class hinged more on Erik not being very good at it, than on his genuine beliefs.

A few days after the game of tag, Val and his class sat down for another 'Life Stories with Bragi' as Alex had started calling it. Once again, they were sharing this class with Erik and his band of merry idiots from Thor clan.

"Good morning everyone." Bragi chimed with his usual cheery attitude.

"It's come to my attention that some of you think I talk too much, so today it's gong to be your turn to have your say." He said, wetting his lips with his tongue.

"As I mentioned back in your first class with me, we Norse like to flyte. So that's what you will be doing today. You'll stand in front of your peers and with cadence and rhyme, slaughter your enemy." He said clenching his fist and raising it, as if this was a real battle.

Bragi strode up and down the isles and picked out Erik and Alex to go first. He called them to the stage at the front of the room and had them face each other.

"Ok Erik, begin." Bragi said, taking a seat In the front row and placing his head on his chin.

Erik looked around, a little lost. He obviously had no idea what to do. Alex took this as his opportunity to take the reins and start the match.

"Cat got your tongue, you look really dumb. You love flexing your muscles but maybe flyting's not so fun." Alex said quietly, a sure smile on his face.

Val was surprised, he had no idea that Alex could do poetry. He just didn't seem the type. Erik shook his head and glared at Alex, then coughed once to clear his throat.

"Shut up you little twig. Stop acting like you're big. You and all of Loki's loser's are in need of a good kick." He said, obviously proud of himself. He folded his arms and raised his head, looking at Alex with a scathing sneer.

"Oh, you've finally found your voice? That rhyme was pretty nice. You can look hard all you want but I can see your eyes are moist." Alex retorted, getting into it now as he strode around the stage, flailing his arms confidently.

"Why don't you come over here and say that. I'll snap you in two you little weasel." Erik shouted, clenching his fists.

"I don't think it counts if it doesn't rhyme mate." Alex laughed, folding his arms.

Erik lunged at him but before he could reach Alex, Bragi had jumped into action and tripped Erik. He landed with a hard thud. None of the class had expected that from Bragi. He was so thin and had never shown any interest in actual fighting.

"I think that's enough for one day." Bragi said through a gasp.

"Flyting isn't supposed to lead to a brawl Erik." He said, shaking his head and looking down at the boy on the ground.

He dismissed the class and the Loki boys praised Alex. It was a strange custom and definitely not something that would be seen as cool back in their world, but, when in Rome and all that, Val thought to himself.

As the weeks dragged on Val started to become a more accomplished fighter. He had recently won his first duel against a boy with a similar build to him in the Bragi clan. The Bragi clan wore laced polo shirts of a royal purple, the colour of the arts. Embroidered on their breast pockets and the back of their cloaks was a lute. A clan symbol that was just as on the nose as the hammers adorned by the Thor clan, or so Alex had said.

Despite winning his first fighting victory, Val was still struggling in hand to hand combat and had suffered many embarrassing defeats to Erik Erikson. Who, by comparison, was a natural born warrior and the pride of Thor clan class one.

Erik was a sore loser and since Alex showed him up at flyting he'd had it in for all of the Loki clan's boys. He took every chance he got to shout 'Loki's losers' at them when they entered shared classes, he also seemed to fight twice as hard when in the ring with one of them. It wasn't just Val anymore, as soon as Erik saw a green polo, he lashed out.

Val had barely seen Kassandra since their late night meeting. Their interactions had been limited to stolen glances in the corridors and awkward hand brushes in the occasional sailing class. They had now being shown how to row with proper form in the little boats and had moved on to knots and sails.

The small interactions he had with Kassandra were awkward for Val. She, however, seemed to ooze confidence in these situations, even enjoying them. That being said, she still wouldn't talk to Val for more than thirty seconds at a time when the rest of her clan were around.

Val hated that he saw so little of her but he couldn't risk leaving the castle at night again now he knew the All Father might know what they were doing. After all, he knew that Dean had sat on his throne and impersonated him, so it wasn't beyond the realm of possibilities to assume that he also knew about Val's trip to the starlit lake.

On the up side, Val wasn't falling behind in his other subjects. He was even becoming an accomplished novice sailor now, despite his aversion to modes of transport. Alex, on the other hand, was pretty bad at everything. He still couldn't grasp the subtle art of Nordic runes. He never used the right knots when sailing and even though his voice was never much above a whisper, he didn't seem to be doing too well in Freya's seduction classes either. In fact, the only subjects he wasn't hopeless in was flyting, which Bragi hadn't tried again since the last time, and combat classes.

Alex was fast and he had won most of his duels so far by dodging and getting in quick hits. He still hadn't beaten Erik yet though and both he and Val had suffered more than their fair share of trips to the healers chamber.

Alice was even worse than Val at hand to hand combat. So far she had only fought the other girls, but she was hopeless. She was, however, a very accomplished navigator and had won more than a few glory points for the clan in the sailing lessons. She had also almost completely mastered the Nordic rune language and could now read full books with only minimal help.

She had started spending most of her free periods in the archive. She loved to read, but despite her invitations to join her, Val and Alex hadn't put one toe so much as through the archive door. They would much rather spend their free time laying around and goofing off.

Life continued in this fashion as more rumours spread about missing students and soon snow began to fall on Odinsall. The lake froze over, emitting a beautiful dazzle in the moonlight. The grass became crunchy with frost and the trees of the forest looked like a gigantic field of Christmas trees. Even the castle itself was rather picturesque and the rolling hills and mountains behind the castle became an indistinguishable sea of white.

The students were given their winter unform. This swapped their rough skin trousers for fur lined ones, their boots were also now fur lined. Their cloaks were worn closed to the front and they were given silky smooth Santa style hats in the colours of their various clans. Each hat was lined at the bottom with black fur, in the place where the white of Santa's hat would be. There was also a black fur ball at the end of the hats.

After another typical day of lessons the students of Odinsall convened in the hall, as they had done many times by now, and began tucking into their evening feast.

"Seen much of Kassandra lately?" Alex teased, raising his eyebrows at Val as he piled his plate with food.

"You know I haven't." Val replied, shaking his head irritably.

It still shocked Val just how much Alex managed to eat in one sitting. Anyone else would be fat by now, or at least have put on some muscle if they had the right genetics. Alex, however, looked exactly the same as he always had – skinny.

"You know, she's not the only girl in the school." Alice chimed in, shooting Alex a glace for bringing it up.

"How do you even know if she likes you, you barely know her."

"I just do ok." Val said, his cheeks beginning to turn a deep scarlet.

"Look Alice, you made Val's face match your hair." Alex laughed, pointing at his friends red face.

Val sunk into his seat and smiled that awkward smile one gives when they don't want others to see just how awkward they feel.

There was a familiar crack and All Father appeared in front of his throne once again.

"Good evening young ones." All Father began, opening his long arms towards them.

"As some of you may be aware we are now well into the winter season. I have been conducting some research these last few weeks on the customs of your world and have discovered that soon it will be, what I believe you call, Christmas."

Excited chatter erupted around the hall. No one had realised it was nearly Christmas, in fact most had forgotten that it was even a thing since the realm of the Gods was so different.

"Calm down." All Father laughed.

"We will be holding celebrations for this wonderful time of the year, however we will not be celebrating Christmas per se."

A groan let out throughout the hall as disheartened students returned to their meals.

"Christmas is a holiday that was stolen from the Norse many hundreds of years ago. We called it Yule. At this time in your civilisation's history Christianity was gaining popularity, mostly thanks to the expanse of the Roman empire. There were few pagans left in Europe, but the ones that did remain were fierce warriors and very devout in their belief in the Gods of our realm. Because of this the Christian church decided that adopting some pagan traditions would ease the conversion of the stubborn ones who were left. As such they decided to adopt the tradition of Yule and tell people it was to celebrate the birth of their prophet Jesus Christ. Factually speaking, this Jesus fellow was born in the summer, but the church decided that changing this date would help them accomplish their conversion goals and bring a more common law to the world they knew." All Father explained, clearly he had done some thorough research on the matter.

"I had no idea." Alice said genuinely shocked. She usually knew things, having an uncommon thirst for knowledge, she leant in closer and stared eagerly at All Father.

This sentiment was shared by many in the hall. There were some looks of surprise floating around and a lot of students seemed genuinely interested. That being said, a lot more of them had now completely switched off, Val and Alex included. They got enough lecturers in classes, they didn't need a history lesson whilst they ate. Give it a break, Val though as he returned to his pork chop.

"I hear your surprise young ones." All Father laughed, obviously loving the attention.

"Did you never wonder why you celebrated by decorating trees? To my knowledge there is no mention of this in the Christian scriptures. Fir trees are the scared trees of Baldr, my son who sadly is no longer with us. He was the God of the sun and these evergreen trees are decorated in celebration of the promise of new life to come in the spring. Winter kills many plants and animals, but Baldr's evergreen trees never die." All Father said wistfully, beginning to pace again.

Val noticed a sad glisten in his one eye. He hadn't realised that All Father had children. He wondered where they were and what they were like. Were they all born with one eye too?

"So, this year we will all celebrate Yule! It's customs are not dissimilar from the ones that you are used to.

As such, classes are cancelled for the week. Instead you will make presents for your friends and clansmen and take some time to rest up."

Before he could finish there was a loud cheer from Thor table. Despite his dislike of the clan, Val had to agree. A week of no classes was something he could get behind. He shared a look with Alex who obviously agreed. Alice, however, let out a quiet "aww".

"As the next year begins we will move onto weapons training and Thor has something very exciting planned for you all, but we'll discuss it properly when the time comes." All Father said, stroking his long plaited beard.

"This Friday, hang your hats at the end of your beds and you might just receive a little gift from me as well." All Father winked, then there was a crack and he was gone.

Of course, Val and his friends knew now that this crack was really the hidden entrance to his chamber opening. One of many mysteries still to be solved in the great castle.

"We're going to make presents?" Alex asked nobody in particular.

"That seems like it would be more suited to Bragi clan than us." He moaned, taking a chunk out of a mostly raw steak.

"How very astute of you young Lokison " Said Bragi who had appeared opposite them on the table and was tucking into a turkey leg.

"My clan are hard at work making presents for you all. Tomorrow those presents will be on sale in this very hall." He said.

This guy really loves to rhyme, Val thought to himself.

"Sale? We don't have any money sir." Said Simon, strolling over from higher up the table.

"Ah, you will each be given ten silver coins to spend as you will. Once the market has closed the student from my clan who made the most money will be rewarded by picking the music which our clan will play for you all on Friday eve. See, there's plenty to be had by all." Said Bragi cheerfully, clapping his hands together.

"Well this should be interesting." Dean said, looking at his clansmen and smiling devilishly.

"Definitely." Alex agreed between bites, shooting a smirking, knowing glance at Val.

The group retired for bed, eagerly awaiting the market they would visit in the morning. Val was hopeful that he would be able to find the perfect gift for Kassandra.

The next day the boys awoke early and, with Alice in tow, headed down to breakfast. Everyone ate fast and then left so the market could be set up. Val, Alice and Alex went down to the frozen lake to kill some time.

"Look at the ice on here, it's so thick and shiny." Alice swooned, bending down on the edge of the docks and looking at her reflection.

"Think you'd be able to get out if you fell in." Alex asked, nudging her lightly with his knee.

"You really know how to darken a nice conversation don't you." Alice said haughtily, getting to her feet and moving away from the water's edge.

"Do you think you could skate on it?" Val asked deep in thought.

"Maybe, if you had any skates." Alex shrugged.

Later on the three headed back to the hall just in time for the market. They entered through the large, duel raven doors and stepped into a completely different setting from the one they had left earlier.

Replacing the tables were thatch roofed stores with all kinds of colourful jewellery, clothing, leather bound books and ink sets. There were sweets, sculptures and necklaces adorned with runes. The hall was warm and a sweet scent filled the air. This was the break from classes they all needed.

The three approached the first stand where a slender boy waved his hand and said; "You have coin, John has wares." In a purring, feline-esq voice.

"Don't mind him." Bragi said, appearing from behind the counter.

"He's really gotten into playing the merchant character."

John the merchant was selling runic necklaces made from black stones and carved with a gold writing. The stones were attached to leather strings allowing them to be worn around the neck.

"These are pretty good." Alex said, picking up a rune engraved stone.

"Yeah they're nice, not what I'm looking for though." Val said dismissively and walked off, Alex dropped the stone and followed behind him.

"You coming Alice?" Val called.

"I'll catch up with you later." Alice said as she wandered off into the forest of merchandise.

"And then there were two." Alex said jovially.

Val searched through stores full of the most exquisite jewels, carved tankards and all kinds of sweets.

Eventually he came across a large stall taking pride of place in the middle of the hall. He was shocked, Alex bumped into Val and he too stood stock still with his jaw practically dragging on the fur laden floor.

The boys couldn't believe their eyes. This stall had items from home, items they thought they would never see again. There were football shirts from the premier league. A *Leeds United* Kit, *Arsenal*, *Newcastle* and others hung around the top of the store. On the counter there were *Lego* sets and a hand carved, wooden set of *Monopoly*. It was incredible, little slices of home. Then Val's eyes affixed on an item hanging in the back.

"How much are they?" Val asked, pointing to the item.

"Ten silvers mate, they weren't easy to make." The student merchant replied as he counted a handful of coins from the previous customer.

"But that's all of my silvers." Val said disheartened, looking down at the little pouch he had been given.

"If that's what you want to get her just do it." Alex grinned, patting him on the back.

"You don't have to worry about getting me a present and it's not like you have any other best friends is it?" He laughed.

"What about Alice and Dean and Simon" Val asked, still looking down at his measly pouch.

"You couldn't afford to get everyone a gift anyway, so I'm sure they'll understand." Alex said, now running his hands over a football top.

"Ok I'll take it!" Val said, handing the student merchant all of his silvers.

After that the boys shopped a little longer but quickly ran out of silvers and got bored. They headed back to the residence and rested by the fire for a while before heading to bed.

The next day a very irritated Loki arrived at the residence with one huge tree and a group of smaller ones. There was a tree for the common area and one for each room. Loki clan shared a lazy day together decorating the trees with runes and sparkling cloths provided by Loki.

The tree decorations matched the clan colour scheme of course, with various blacks and greens thrown haphazardly into the mix. Loki had even made little figures of himself to sit atop the numerous trees, despite pretending not to enjoy the festivities.

The next day and night there was heavy snowfall so on Wednesday the entire clan spent the morning having a boys versus girls snowball fight. Dean, naturally, aimed all of his snowballs strategically in the hopes of getting one down a girls top. However, this dastardly plan was cut short when Alice cottoned onto his scheme, told the rest of the girls and they threw a volley of snowballs at him, aiming below the waist.

"Snowballs indeed." Alex had said to him, holding his stomach as he laughed.

The rest of the week continued similarly and the students enjoyed a week of generic winter activities, lots of rest and plenty of lavish feasting.

Finally Friday arrived and the students were treated to a large feast of duck and turkey. The celebration lasted late into the night and as the week drew to a close, no one was fretting over the missing pupils anymore. It was a perfect distraction from a concerning situation.

That night, before everyone went to bed, they hung their hats on the end of their beds as instructed by All Father. The boys were all exhausted and quickly fell asleep.

Later that night Val awoke, feeling a presence in the room. He sat up and saw a dark figure sneaking across the foot of his bed. Scared stiff, he sat for what felt like a while and stared at the figure which was now unmoving.

"Go back to sleep young Val, you don't want to wake the others this late." Said a familiar and warm voice.

As Val's eyes adjusted to the darkness he realised that it was All Father dressed in a green and brown Santa costume.

"Why are you dressed like Santa?" Val whispered, screwing up his eyes to see better in the darkness.

"Santa dresses like me!" All Father whispered indignantly.

"Your Santa Clause is actually modelled on earlier myths of me placing fruit into the boots of the Norse during Yule." He said, continuing to put things in the boys hats.

"Were the myths true?" Val yawned.

"Who knows." The All Father winked and then crept towards the door and left the room.

Val carefully stood up and walked to the window to get a mug of water which he had left there when, once again he saw a strange light. This time it wasn't disappearing, it was much closer to the castle and was heading in the direction of the forest.

Val squinted for a better view and could just about make out the shape of a person. He stood at the window for a minute and watched as the dimly lit figure disappeared behind the forest's foliage.

The next morning a tired Val was woken up by Alex, who jumped on his bed laughing, whilst he was still in it.

"Have you seen this, our hats are full!" Alex said elated, swinging his hat around like a lasso and still jumping on Val's bed.

Val groggily sat up and looked at Alex who was showing him a set of well-made playing cards in his outstretched hand. On these cards, some of the Gods had replaced the characters. All Father was the King, Freya the Queen, Thor the Jack and...

"Oh my god is that Loki as the Joker?" Dean laughed looking at his own deck.

Val checked his hat and it seemed he too had received a finely made set of cards. Dean and Simon decided to exchange gifts and both had bought a gift for the other. Simon gave Dean some weird looking Norse sweets in the shape of dragons and Dean gave Simon some Norse chocolate's in the shape of shields. The two then left for the common area and for breakfast as Alex waited for Val to get dressed.

"I got you something by the way." Alex said, digging around in his trunk.

"I thought we weren't doing gifts?" Val said as he pulled on his, now empty hat.

"No, I told you not to get me one so you could give one to your crush. I never said I wasn't getting you one. Besides, who else would I buy for." Alex said smiling.

Alex handed Val a thin, soft package wrapped in brown paper. Val tore it open and saw a vintage yellow *Leeds United* shirt from the 90's.

"How did you get this!" Val said amazed, holding the shirt up for a better view.

"It was at that shop where you bought your present. It's not a real one but I think the lad did a good job recreating it." Alex said, smiling at Val.

"Thanks mate this is awesome. I used to go to the matches with my dad when I was a little kid." Val said.

The football games were the only real memories he had of his Dad. He remembered the buzzing crowds and being high up in the stands so the players were barely bigger than those on a foosball table.

The two boys shared a silent moment, remembering the loved ones they had lost when they were transported to Odinsall, and before.

"Come on lets go see if Alice is dressed yet, I need to give her a gift too." Alex said, grabbing Val's arm and shoving him out of the room.

"I didn't even think you and Alice got on that well." Val laughed as he was forced into the common area.

"Well we're not best mates or anything, but other than you she's probably the person I spend the most time with." Alex shrugged.

In the warm common area Alice was sat by the fireplace looking through her own set of Norse Gods playing cards.

"You got some too then?" Val asked as he leant on the arm of her arm chair.

"It looks like everyone did." Alice smiled looking up at the two boys.

"Merry Yule." Alex said cheerily passing Alice a small parcel.

"Merry Yule?" Val said mockingly.

"Doesn't quite have the same ring to it as Christmas does it?"

"You got me something." Alice said surprised, receiving the gift.

"Thank you." She smiled, ripping open the small package to reveal a carved wooden box. Inside the box were a pair of silver stud earrings with little wolves carved into them.

"These are beautiful!" She exclaimed as she started putting them on.

"You really didn't have to. I got something for you both as well." She said, pulling out two small packages of brown paper wrapped in a bow of string.

Both boys took the presents offering their thanks and opened them revealing two identical necklaces. The necklaces were smooth black pebbles with a golden compass looking rune carved into them. The rune looked like a plus sign with an X placed over the top of it. On the end of each line were various patterns making each end look like a unique trident.

"Wow these are really cool." Alex said, pulling his over his head.

"They're called vegvisir, it's a rune that brings good luck when travelling. I thought it was kind of fitting since we all travelled here." She smiled.

"Is that what you were doing when you disappeared at the market?" Alex asked, now fiddling with his new necklace.

"Maybe." Alice winked.

"What's wrong?" She asked noticing that Val had gone quiet.

"N-nothing, I just feel bad cause I didn't get you guys anything. I spent all my money on a gift for Kassandra." Val said sadly as he looked down at his necklace laying limp in his palm.

"I didn't get you it expecting one in return you know." Alice said kindly as she placed a hand on his arm.

"Though it wouldn't kill you to remember that she's not the only girl in your life." Alice teased.

The three went down to breakfast and enjoyed more turkey, toast and bacon. About halfway through their meal the winner of the merchants market was announced as the boy who made the replica's from the human world. He proudly stood in front of Bragi house, who all had instruments in hand and they played and sung a rendition of *Last Christmas* but replaced the word Christmas with Yule.

By the end of the song the whole hall had joined in to belt out Last Yule and the place felt full of joy. As students started to move around, Val got up from his seat at the Loki table and gingerly walked over to the Freya table, gift in hand. He approached Kassandra nervously as she chatted to her attractive, intimidating girlfriends.

"Happy Yule Kassandra." Val said, trying to sound aloof.

"Don't open it until later." He said passing her a large brown package tied with string. Under the string was a letter.

Val then left hastily and re-joined his friends at the table.

"Did she like it?" Alice asked as she surgically sliced her bacon.

"I told her not to open it till later." Val shrugged.

"He asked her out on a date and didn't want to get rejected in public." Alex laughed, digging him in the ribs with his knuckled.

"How do you know?" Val replied, staring at Alex with a slack jaw.

"You're not the only one who doesn't sleep straight away mate, I read that letter over your shoulder as you wrote it." Alex said, grinning.

"Oh Kassandra, where art thou Kassandra." Alex sang, holding his hands to his chest and doing his best impression of an actor in a play.

"Ooh a love letter." Alice teased, raising her eyebrows at Val.

The teasing continued for a little while but eventually the three returned to the residence common area. Whilst they were sat around talking Val remembered the figure in the forest from the night before.

"Last night I got woken up when All Father was delivering those cards and I swear I saw a person holding a light walking towards the forest." Val told the other two as they all sat in the leather chairs, getting warmed by the fire.

"That's a bit odd." Alice remarked, looking over at him.

"It gets stranger." Val said, now standing in front of them.

"It's not the first time I've seen a light go into the forest at night. I've seen it a few times since we got here, always late at night and once it gets to the tree line it disappears." Val said, gesticulating like he was delivering a presentation.

"I thought no one was allowed in the forest after dark?" Alex said through a yawn.

"We're definitely not, but I doubt the Gods have to abide by the same rules we do." Alice said thoughtfully.

"I bet it was Loki." Alex replied, swinging his legs onto the arm of the chair and sliding down to a slumped position.

"There's always been something about that guy that didn't sit well with me."

"Well, it was hard to tell, but I had a feeling it was a man, so it could have been." Val shrugged.

The three pondered a little more and expressed their shared distrust of Loki before retiring to bed, bidding farewell to the Yule period.

Chapter 9

WEAPONS WEEK

Val awoke the next morning to a fresh timetable and clan meeting before breakfast. Loki explained to them that this week would be all about an introduction to weapons training as they had an event coming up where they would need to use them.

Despite pestering from Dean, Loki wouldn't reveal what the event was but said he had a special and exclusive lesson for his clan that he hoped would keep them from losing too many glory points.

The first lesson was Archery class with Freya. Loki clan shared this class with Bragi clan and the group was marched down into the forest for the first time. Val was oddly uneasy in the forest, despite it looking like any typical wood you might find back in the human world. He wondered if this uneasy feeling was a product of the recurring light he had seen, as he trapsed over fallen leaves and branches.

After a short walk they arrived in a clearing. The students grouped up near a rack of bows. Opposite them was an array of targets ranging from the kind you would see at a county fair, to the kind you would expect *Katniss Everdeen* to annihilate in *The Hunger*

Games. Some of the targets were elaborate and looked like they would be able to move as well.

"Ok everyone, go grab a bow and a quiver and line up in front of me." Freya commanded cheerfully, standing in front of the group.

The class did as they were asked and lined up single file. Val couldn't help but notice that these were compound bows with pully systems at the top and the bottom. Freya, noticing the puzzled look on more than one of the students faces, said:

"What, were you expecting wooden longbows? I bet you think we treat injuries with leeches too right?" She laughed, placing her hands on her hips.

"Did you honestly think that as humanity created new technologies, that we Gods didn't progress alongside you?" She said indignantly, shaking her windswept hair out of her face.

Even with messy, tussled hair she looked amazing. Val had never noticed before but she wore a golden ring on her upper arm, just below her shoulder. It accented the delicately etched separation of her toned muscles, like an ancient Greek statue.

"It's more that we're living in a castle, sailing longboats and there's no wi-fi, but you draw the line on modern bows?" Dean laughed, lifting his palms upwards, questioningly.

"War is a Norse' lifeblood young Dean." Freya smiled, she walked towards him and bent down slightly to look him the eyes.

"Modern technology is important in the art of battle." She stroked his face gently and he blushed for the first time since arriving at the castle.

Val noticed that, though she was looking at his eyes, that's not where he was looking. If Freya had realised, she wasn't showing it. Maybe she didn't care, she's probably used to being ogled, Val thought.

"Then why are there no guns?" Alice asked, innocently raising her hand as she spoke.

"Because there is no honour in an easily won fight." Freya said smugly, turning her back on Dean and returning to the front of the class, her hips swaying as she walked.

"But aren't guns just as hard to master as a bow?" Simon asked from the side of Val.

"Erm." Freya stuttered, placing her hand on her chin and stroking an imaginary beard.

"There just aren't any guns ok. Now gather round and listen to what I'm about to say." Freya said, recovering from her glaring lack of knowledge.

"Hold the bow out straight and place your first three fingers under where the arrow would sit. Now you pull that string back past your cheek and move the bow with your eyes to look where you want the arrow to go, adjusting for the arrow falling time." She said, miming the actions as she explained.

"The rest is practice and instinct, so grab your arrows, take your positions and let fly."

The students scattered, all moving towards the buckets of arrows placed near the firing line. Val picked up a handful of arrows and took up position next to Alice and Alex. He held the bow as instructed, pulled back the string past his cheek, looked at the closest target in his direct line of sight and let go. The arrow whizzed through the air and struck the target somewhere near the outer ring.

Not too shabby for a first try, he thought. He then looked across at Alice's target which now had two arrows sticking close to the bullseye.

"Well done my little scarlet marksmen!" Freya applauded.

"You might just be a natural at this." She sung in a high pitched voice as she carried pacing up and down the line of student archers.

Alice turned a deep shade of red matching her hair and awkwardly thanked Freya for her praise, though she had already moved on to another student.

The class continued practicing for a while and Val got his first bullseye. Alex, however, was hopeless. So far he had only hit the target twice and both times were in the outer ring. He'd sent most of his arrows flying somewhere into the trees behind.

Archery came to a finish and the class moved on to their next weapons class: axe's with Thor. This class was also taught in the forest in a clearing near to the archery clearing and as they passed a sneering Thor clan, Val realised that these introductory weapons classes were being taught in a round robin . The axe practice space was set up like a battle arena with wooden dummies scattered around the area.

"Ah, younglings. Today begins your axe training." Thor boomed, producing an axe with an intricately carved and varnished wooden handle. Sitting atop the carved handle was a glinting steel axe head with one side sharpened to a point more like a tomahawk.

"This is a modern bearded axe." Thor said, holding his weapon out for the students to see.

"Today you will get a feel for the axe, hit some dummies, throw the axe if you like. Then later we will practice parrying, and the strongest of you may get the opportunity to wield two axe's at once."

Alex's quiet eyes shone with a mean glint. The group began practicing and Alex was like a man possessed, chopping targets and pretending to dodge. He even got in a pretty good throw once or twice.

Alice, on the other hand, struggled to lift her axe, let alone do any real damage. It seemed that archery would be her favoured style of combat.

Val did ok, towards the end of the class he felt relatively comfortable holding and hitting with the axe. However, he had terrible throwing aim and at one point nearly shaved Thor's head with it, accidentally, of course.

The next day, sore from the physical activity of axe handling, the class tried their hands at being spearmen. Taught by Bragi, this class was all about thrusting and parrying and trying not to get it stuck in the sandbag men they used as targets.

Val excelled at this and thoroughly enjoyed himself as he attacked sandbag after sandbag and imagined he was laying siege to a castle where Erik was the ruler.

Alex and Alice exchanged a quiet smile at seeing their friend actually enjoy a lesson for once as usually Val was quiet and laid back and didn't seem to care much about any of the subjects they were being taught.

The week continued as the students stabbed, thrusted and slashed their way through session after session. By Friday everyone was thoroughly exhausted, with sagging shoulders and aching muscles. At meal time Alex was eating even more than usual, though he still never bulked out.

After dinner, when all of Loki clan were ready to collapse in bed, they climbed through the shield door and were met with none other than the trickster God himself. He was stood in front of the fire place with a wheeled in blackboard and chalk.

"Sit. It's time for that special lesson I promised you." He grinned menacingly.

"This eve I am going to teach you about basic strategy and battle tactics. You'll come to know the importance of this later on, but for now just listen, and if you fall asleep." He said staring at Dean meanly.

"I will wake you in a most unpleasant way." He smirked and mimed a throwing action, still keeping eye contact with Dean.

Loki went on to discuss numerous tactics such as a pincer movement: where some of your army fight the enemy head on whilst the others circle around and attack from behind. He carried on late into the night, throwing multiple hardbacked books at Dean and Alex, who couldn't stay awake no matter how hard they tried.

Both boys were covered in deep red bruises from the heavy hardbacks they'd been pelted with. They both grumbled their dislike for their clan leader but despite the pain, they were still too exhausted to even complain properly.

Finally, when It was good and late and everyone had a headache, Loki left, wheeling his blackboard with him. Then, everyone went gladly to sleep.

The weekend passed and weapons week was over. On Monday classes resumed as normal with weapons lessons interspersed among their usually classes. After lunch on Monday, Val and the others had history class with Mimir. He was an old god, frail looking with shaved grey hair and an unruly grey beard. They had had many history classes with him by now but this one was particularly interesting.

Mimir taught the students about the Jotun. They were a race of frost giants who had partaken in countless wars with the Gods and were their sworn enemy. They lived in Jotunheim, a world of ice and snow and legend had it that they envied the Gods for having such fertile soil and a temperate climate to live in.

After class, Alex, Alice and Val took a walk towards the lake. It was cold out and you could see their breath. Alex pretended he was smoking, miming the action of pulling a cigarette from his lips, that is until Alice slapped him on the back of the head and told him to grow up.

"I was in the archive the other day and I swear a read a book which said Loki's father was a Jotun." Alice said, deep in thought.

"What!" Val and Alex said in unison, both turning to look at her as they walked.

"Aren't they the bad guys?" Val asked, already forgetting most of what Mimir had told them.

It wasn't that Val disliked history class. He just struggled to concentrate sometimes and Mimir wasn't the most engaging teacher. A typical class with him involved the students sitting down and taking notes whilst he lectured them. Val hated being talked at. His stories were usually, kind of interesting, it was just that they weren't engaging enough.

"Yes, we literally just learnt about them and how they want to take over this realm." Alice sighed, shaking her head at him.

"Makes sense I guess, he's always ice cold towards us." Alex said, grinning, obviously proud of his joke.

"We should keep an eye on him then." Val said, resolute.

"I've been telling you there was something odd about him from the start." Alex said, glancing at Val who was now staring out over the lake.

Chapter 10

STARS ON THE ICE

The next day whilst at breakfast Kassandra hurried past the Loki clan table and dropped a small piece of parchment on Val's plate. The parchment said; "midnight?" Alex and Alice had both noticed this, though no one else at the table had. The two leaned in to talk to a blushing Val in hushed whispers so they weren't overheard.

"What does it say?" Alex asked, looking over Val's shoulder who had now folded the parchment and was tucking it inside his cloak.

"Midnight?" Val replied, failing at hiding his glee.

"So you're really doing this then?" Alice asked disapprovingly shaking her head at him.

"Even after the warning All Father gave us?" She folded her arms in protest.

"Some rules are made to be broken Alice, I got her that Yule gift especially for this." Val replied sharply, irritated by his friend's lack of enthusiasm.

"I know you did mate." Alex said calmly, attempting to mediate.

"But just be careful, we don't know how much All Father can see. After all, he knew about Dean sitting on his throne."

Val thought back to Dean's imitation of All Father on the night they snuck out to see him. He still wondered if All Father had known about his last meet up with Kassandra. If he did, he'd kept it to himself.

"Well. After tonight we'll know." Val said defensively.

"Besides, he'd have found Tom and the other missing students by now if he was that all-seeing." He added defiantly.

Tom and a myriad of other students were still missing. Though no one really talked about it anymore, Val was sure it was still in the back of people's minds – especially Dean and Simon who were close with Tom.

"For all we know he has found them. No one has gone missing in weeks now." Alice retorted.

She was right, since the night they met with All Father there had been no new rumours of students going missing.

"Anyway, enough depressing talk. Let's just get through today and see what happens tonight eh?" Val said with a vacant look, realising that he was on the verge of crossing the line by bringing up the missing students. This topic, though less prominent, was still a cause of worry after all – especially to those who were close with the missing.

The three spent a relatively normal and uneventful day in classes. Val was nervous and spent most of the lecturers biting his nails and shaking his leg, irritating Alice to no end. Alice took her studies seriously, a trait she had carried from their old world, to this one.

That evening, once Dean and Simon had fallen asleep, Val headed out as Alex, who had stayed up, wished him luck. He also made Val promise to tell him all the gossip when he got back.

Val crept down the now familiar corridor and into the dark, empty hall. He opened the raven doors and walked down towards the lake where he had asked Kassandra to meet him in the letter he had given her, along with her present at Yule.

He noticed that it was a full moon tonight and the iced over lake glistened like the shimmering stars above. He couldn't have asked for a more romantic setting. As he reached the lake he saw Kassandra shadowed against the dock, waiting.

"Why am I always the first one here." She said playfully, twirling her golden locks.

"Probably because my residence is the furthest away from the exit." Val laughed nervously but trying to seem unphased.

Kassandra moved in to hug Val. At first he was stiff to her embrace, arms pencil-like down by his sides, but her warmth enveloped him and he wearily lifted them up and wrapped them delicately around her waist. He wasn't sure where or how to hold her. He'd never been this close to a girl before. He could smell the soft scent of rosemary swirling around her hair, it was intoxicating. Val could have stayed like that forever, but her touch was fleeting and Kassandra moved to disentangle herself from him.

"Thank you so much for the present Val!" She said sincerely, the curve of her smile highlighting dimples in her cheeks.

She moved back over to the dock and crouched down, rooting around in the medium sized box that Val had given her. She looked up at him kindly and removed two pairs of boots with sharp blades attached to the sole. They were handcrafted ice skates, this was what Val had spent his allotment of silver on at the Yule merchant market.

Kassandra offered a pair to Val as she sat on the hard, wooden dock and began pulling her pair on. As she did this her skirt lifted just a little and Val caught himself staring at her soft looking skin. He bashfully looked away and hoped the moonlight wouldn't reveal his flushed face. He sat on the side of the dock and pulled on his own skates.

"It's a good job the lake is still frozen over." Kassandra said, carefully lacing up her skate.

"Have you ever skated before?"

"Honestly no." Val admitted, still struggling to get the first one on his foot.

"But I remembered you talked about it once at show and tell back when we were in primary school." He said, remembering the confident and well-travelled young girl he once shared a classroom with.

"I can't believe you can remember that!" Kassandra said, stopping what she was doing and turning to look at him.

"You'd barely even spoken a word to me until we arrived here."

"I was always too nervous to talk to you. You were always surrounded by people and I don't always do too well in crowds." Val said quietly, reflecting on the social inadequacies he had struggled with his entire life.

"You didn't seem to have a problem asking the All Father about our parents on the first day and that was in front of everyone." She said confrontationally. She shone a cheeky grin at Val through the dark, but he didn't see it.

"That was different, I was angry and confused and, I don't know, it just came out." Val said defensively, pulling apart the leather of the skate to loosen its laces.

"Well I liked that confidence." Kassandra said, gracefully slipping off the dock and onto the icy lake.

"Come on, I'll show you how to use these skates." She said, performing a twirl and beckoning to him to join her.

Val edged himself off of the dock and onto the ice, holding onto the wooden planks for dear life. He felt like *Bambi*, feet slipping despite his best efforts to stand still. He started wondering if the skates were a good idea after all. He might just end up embarrassing himself in front of Kassandra.

"Come here, take my hands and I'll guide you out." She giggled, taking both his hands in hers.

Val was acutely aware that his hands were a bit clammy. Kassandra slid carefully backwards, taking Val with her as she kept him steady and guided him towards the centre of the deeply frozen lake. Then, suddenly, she let go and Val was moving on his own.

"That's it!" She cheered, clapping her hands together.

"Now lift yours legs like an exaggerated walk and lean into it. Let the momentum keep you going." She said encouragingly, lifting her hands to her mouth as she spoke, like a human megaphone.

Val did as Kassandra instructed, if a little shakily. Soon he was moving in circles and Kassandra clapped even harder. He turned towards her, grinning, when a panicked thought came over him:

"How do I stop!?"

He was about to shout this question to Kassandra but it was too late. The two collided and fell to the ground, hard. They were an entangled mess of legs and arms. Val's knee had gone dead where he hit his funny bone though if Kassandra was hurt, she wasn't showing it. She started laughing and Val joined in, partly relieved.

They laid facing together, half holding each other for what seemed like an age - but was probably only about thirty seconds. Val looked deep into her soft eyes, glinting like the Caribbean sea at sunrise. He had always loved her eyes, for as long as he could remember. He read somewhere once that they were the portal to the soul and he believed that Kassandra's far outmatched his own.

Though he had never really spoken to her before their arrival at Odinsall, he had long being an admirer of her charm and confidence. They say that people often look to others to fill in the gaps of their own personality traits and perhaps this was the reason that Val saw confidence as such a desirable quality in another. He had never been a confident person. He was the grey man. Destined to be the supporting character in his own story, or so he thought.

"Always the bridesmaid, never the bride." A phrase his mother used to regurgitate when her dates went badly. Val felt like it kind of fit him too though. Maybe it was in his blood.

Even without her good looks, Kassandra would have always stood out. A personality like hers could take over the world. She was ambitious and capable, a dangerous mix. She had been captain of the volleyball team in her old life and people had always flocked to her. Though her beauty could topple an empire of course. Wars have been waged for less.

"What's that look?" She asked softly, glancing at his lips.

"Nothing." Val said brushing off the question, realising he'd spaced out.

"Ok." She said, staring at him through the glow of the stars.

"Listen, Kas-" Val started, but he was interrupted by a loud cawing sound.

Val sat up quickly, heart thumping and looking around for the source of the noise. It was one of All Father's raven's by the look of it, flying low, above them.

"What a romantic evening." A slow, sneeringly sarcastic voice said from the darkness.

Kassandra jumped, taking in a quick inhale of breath, and now both of them were sat up looking around for the source of the voice.

"You best come back to shore. You two are in a lot of trouble." The taunting voice said.

Val wasn't sure what to do at first but before he could make a decision, Kassandra stood up and grabbed Val's hands helping him to his feet. She guided the two of them back to the dock where Loki, the source of the voice stood. His cruel smile was all that could be seen on his black silhouette, shadowed by the moonlight.

They both climbed onto the dock and began changing their footwear, neither uttering a word.

"Once you've changed your shoes I think we'll have to have a little conversation in my chambers." Loki said menacingly, licking his thin lips.

They changed their shoes and got to their feet. Loki beckoned them to follow him and they did so, silently trapsing behind him.

Val stole a quick glance at Kassandra who was staring straight ahead. She didn't seem worried. Did she not know Loki? Maybe she just didn't care about getting in trouble. After all, she hadn't asked to be here, none of them had. Still though, the Gods were powerful and being on their bad side probably wasn't for the best.

Loki lead them through the large raven doors and through the corridor, heading towards the Loki clan rooms. Just before the shield door, he took a sharp left turn. They were facing a large painting of a frosted wasteland.

"Jotunheim." Val thought, a cold shiver sliding down his spine.

Loki put his hand behind the painting and it swung inwardly, revealing an entrance. Loki lead them inside and into a sparsely furnished office room. The walls had but one decoration, a large portrait of Loki looking regal and wearing a thin crown of gold with stag like horns protruding from the top of it. There was a fancy wooden desk in front of this painting and Loki moved behind it sitting on a cushioned chair.

"So, think you're above the All Father's rules do you?" He said coldly, curling his fingers together.

"N-no sir." Val replied instinctively. He stood stiffly, arms pinned to his side.

"No? It certainly doesn't seem that way when I catch the two of you galivanting on the lake in the hours of darkness." He said sharply, looking between the two of them with a piercing glare.

Val didn't know what to do for the best. He was completely at the whims of this egotistical maniac. Worse still, so was Kassandra.

"It's my fault sir." Kassandra said suddenly, stepping forward and bringing her hands to her chest.

"I asked Val to come. The skates were mine, it was all my idea."

"Kassandra no-" Val began, reaching out to her.

"Be quite." Loki said forcefully, looking at Val with his cruel eyes.

Val lowered his outreaching hand slowly and fell silent. He looked longingly at Kassandra who was stood in front of hm, to his right. She was ahead of him and he could no longer see her eyes. Her fists were now down by her sides and clenched. He noticed a slight tremor and despite the awful situation they were in, he couldn't help but admire her guts.

"I will take this under consideration girl. I know all too well how irresistible the charms of a daughter of Freya can be. But be that as it may, even though he is in my clan, I cannot let Val off the hook with such a brazen lack of respect for rules." Loki said nastily. He took a breath, cracked his knuckles and continued.

"Val, you have lost our clan glory points today, and be thankful that is your only punishment." He said, sighing.

"Girl, you are to report to me before bed every evening for the next month. I have plenty of difficult tasks I need completing and making you my servant for a while should be a suitable punishment." He grinned, looking her up and down slowly.

His words and that perverse looking stare sent a shiver down Val's spine. A burning rage was bubbling inside his chest, but he had to push it down. He knew he'd only make things worse if he stood up to Loki now.

He'd already lost his chance to play the hero, a chance Kassandra hadn't passed up. He didn't deserve her. How could he ever be worthy of a girl like that. He'd let her take the fall for something that was his idea. He was worthless and he knew it. He stared at the ground, not daring to look at her.

Loki delivered Val back to the shield door and led Kassandra away towards her own clan's residence. Val looked up suddenly and stole one last, painful glance at Kassandra as she was led away. For just a moment, their eyes locked and he could tell that she was scared. Despite this she smiled a brave smile at him and then she was gone.

He felt even worse. She was putting on a brave face for him. What expression had he pulled at her to merit that kind of reaction?

Val opened the shield door and retired to his bed feeling utterly defeated. Alex was asleep when Val returned so he decided to tell him about it in the morning. Val laid motionlessly atop the bed furs that night until the crack of dawn came.

He then fell into a disturbed sleep.

Chapter 11

BATTLE PLAN

The next day Val told Alex and Alice about the nights events over breakfast. Alice wasn't best pleased and showed her disapproval, crossing her arms and scowling – it was a look she was giving Val more and more these days. He deserved it.

Alex, however, was more sympathetic. He could tell his friend was upset and decided not to say anything to make it worse, reassuring Val that it wasn't a big deal in his quiet and calming voice.

This sentiment was not shared by the rest of his clan who soon heard the news that Val had lost them a considerable amount of glory points. The older students in particular were not best pleased as they had all being trying their best to raise the clan's ranking out of last place, a feat which now seemed almost impossible. Thor clan had the lead by a considerable amount and even Bragi clan, third in the running, were now fifty points ahead of Loki clan.

Over the next few days Val noticed heated glares from his clan and the common area became an uncomfortable and unwelcoming place for him. He started spending his free time in the boy's room, doing his best to avoid his upper clansmen. Luckily,

Dean and Simon didn't seem to care too much and they were both still the same as they ever were around Val. They did, however spend less time around him in public, not wanting to become social pariahs like he now was.

It didn't take long for the news of his night time escapades to reach the ears of the other clans. Erik consistently made a point of mentioning, loudly and obnoxiously, how Val had single handily ruined Loki's losers chances of a comeback. Erik took a cruel pleasure in humiliating Val, flashing his teeth through a sadistic smile as he berated him.

Alex's advice was to ignore him, but that was easier said than done.

The days turned into weeks and Val hadn't spoken to Kassandra since. He wondered if she was avoiding him as every time he caught sight of her she would disappear within her group of Freya girls. He couldn't even get near her in sailing classes, which Loki clan shared with Freya clan.

He'd messed up and he knew it. His dislike of Loki grew more with each passing day as he began blaming him for the situation he now found himself in. His two best friends, Alex and Alice, were the only thing getting him through these hard times.

In assassination class Val would sit at the back, staring daggers at Loki. A class he was once good at became a personal lesson in hiding his feelings. He was starting to get pretty good at pushing his anger further down. The bubbling hatred was now in his stomach, forced downwards from his chest.

He was completely demotivated in lessons and due to his average nature, if he wasn't trying he wasn't going to do very well. Loki's class was his top subject, but now the idea of being anything like the trickster God made him feel sick. He had lost interest in performing well.

As the weeks dragged on and Val was shunned, winter turned into spring and the lake defrosted. One morning whilst at breakfast the all familiar crack of All Father shook the hall. He had an announcement.

"Good morning. As we enter the spring we are going to be holding some inter-clan, class events. At the beginning of next week we will start the raid battles!" He said excitedly, clicking his fingers and refilling everyone's tankards with honey mead.

"Your clan leaders will explain these in more detail later, for now though I want to announce the pairings." He said, producing his Santa style hat with a devilish grin.

"We'll start with class one."

He reached his long, thin hand into the hat and dug around. He twisted his wrist and stirred the inner contents of the hat. Eventually, after some considerable rummaging he produced four scraps of parchment, one after the other. He dropped the hat and held two scraps in each hand.

"Pairing one will be Loki and Bragi clans vs Freya and Thor clans. You will battle on Tuesday. That gives you three days to prepare." He said, holding up three fingers and showing them to the four tables.

He then began drawing parchment lots for the other classes and revealing their match ups. He finished by telling the clans that there would be a prize of one hundred glory points to the battle winners. Then, with another loud crack, he disappeared.

This could be Val's chance to end his exile and turn his dire social standing on its head. He looked at Alex who stared back at him mischievously. Obviously he was thinking the same thing. There was just one problem. Val sucked at fighting.

He was weak, scrawny and though he had improved a lot since the term began, he was still miles behind Erik. The bully who would be on the opposing team. As if he knew Val was thinking about him, Erik started chanting "Loki's losers" from his table and pretty son half of his clan had joined in. The chorus rang out across the hall.

Facing Thor clan was going to be a tough challenge. Even tougher was the prospect of fighting Kassandra, or any girl for that matter. If there was one thing Val knew for sure it was that he was going to need an edge. Something to make him stand out in the battle and help him win back the favour of his clan.

The day dragged on and Val was lost in thought. He couldn't concentrate on his lessons, not that he had been a good student the last few weeks anyway. He had a goal and it made him feel better pondering how to achieve it, rather than skulking around his clanmates.

Alice had spent much of the day trying to brainstorm for Val and help him gain his edge. However, this was a fruitless endeavour. Val was simply too average to become a stand out in just three days. It was hopeless and the more Val thought on his situation, the more he began to realise this.

Come nightfall Val was utterly defeated. He dragged himself into the residence as Alex tried fruitlessly to cheer him up. He cracked jokes like it was his job, some of them were actually quite good. The problem was Val, he'd been in a terrible mood for weeks and the prospect of his looming defeat just made it worse.

Looking up from his portrait of self-pity, Val saw his clan crowded around a central figure in the common area.

It was Loki. Of course, as if Val needed another reason not to want to be in the common area. Loki had a superior grin on his face and as the last of the stragglers entered the room, he began to speak.

"Be silent and listen well. You all share a piece of me within you. In your personality and your affinities. So what I'm about to say is of upmost importance to you." He said, head raised, adopting the regal stance from the portrait in his chambers.

"Shame we don't share his inflated self-worth." Alex whispered sarcastically.

Val was only half paying attention to Loki, his mind still struggling to find a solution to his problem.

"I taught you basic tactics last time we had a meeting." Loki continued, tapping his fingers on the blackboard he had brought once again.

"I did this to sow the seed of thought over fighting. You all take after me, so raw power will not be on your side in battle. It is the ability to outwit your opponent that will turn the tides in your favour. Use your cunning and trick the enemy into giving you the advantage." He grinned and for a second Val almost thought he actually cared about how well they did.

"Outwit your opponent." Val repeated in his head. Maybe that's how he could stand out from the crowd, by tricking the enemy. Thor clan weren't exactly known for their brains. How to achieve this would be another hurdle in itself though.

"How are we supposed to do that then?" Dean asked from somewhere near the back of the room.

"What do you take me for?" Loki riled, opening his hand as if to magic a book into it but deciding against it.

"I'm not your mother, work it out yourself."

Loki then began to walk towards the shield door, forcing the clan to part for him. He reached the door and stopped for a moment. He turned and said:

"You better not lose."

He then opened the door and disappeared into the dark corridor, his cloak swishing casually behind him.

Alice wasn't at breakfast the next morning. The students had been given the next two days off in order to hone their skills before the competition. Alex and Val spent most of the day brainstorming strategy ideas. However, they hadn't gotten very far.

Val knew his clan well enough to understand their strengths and he knew that to trick the brutish Thor clan he would have to utilise individual strengths. The issue was the cunning part, how could he come up with a devilish plan when he'd never seen the battlefield?

That evening in the hall, Alice finally showed up. She looked exhausted, she was covered in dust and dirt and her hair was a mess with twigs and leaves sticking out in place. She was a long way away from that cute girl Val had met a few months ago.

"I might have some information that'll help you Val." Alice said, breathing heavily as if she had been running.

Val raised his head from his plate and looked at Alice. He saw that her face was flushed and her hair was a mess. She was covered in mud and in need of a bath, he thought.

"Jesus, what happened to you?" Alex laughed through a mouthful of bread.

"Never mind that." Alice said, starting to catch her breath.

"I know what the setting of the raid battle is going to be." She said, smiling proudly.

The two boys eagerly leaned in and Alice filled them in on the layout and location of the battle. Pretty soon a scheme was hatched.

The next day passed in relative peace and it was game time. There was a nervous air at breakfast that morning as the rest of the students got ready to watch class one battle it out. The raid battle was going to take place in front of the whole school, a fact that Alice realised due to the location she had discovered. All Father had announced this before breakfast, but the trio were already aware and prepared.

The clans of class one were escorted onto the docks and split into their teams. All four of the clan leaders took their places in front of the class as the spectators boarded the longboats and sailed ahead. After they were safely out of earshot, the briefing began.

"We won't labour on pleasantries this morning." Thor began, serious for once.

"The raid is simple. One team invades from the water, the other defends the camp. How you do this is up to you. The winner will be decided by the last man, or team, standing."

This was no surprise to Val as Alice had already guessed that this would be the format and told him so. He was as ready as he could have been.

"We have crafted you special weapons for this task." Freya said, her luscious, shinning lips inviting the boy's gazes.

"You can use any weapons you want and as many as you want. There are axes, spears, hammers, swords, daggers and bows available for this contest. They're a little different from what you are used to though." She sniggered, lifting her hand to cover her mouth. Val thought this was kind of cute, a word he wouldn't normally have used to describe her.

Bragi then bent down and opened a large chest. Inside the chest were black weapons and a plethora of large tins.

"These weapons are made of hardened rubber. They'll hurt but they won't maim or kill you." Bragi reassured, picking up a black spear to show them. He pulled the tip of the spear with his finger and, with a little effort, it bent and then sprang back into place when he let go.

"The tins have paint in them. One tin per clan, the colours match the clan colours. Obviously. If even a drop of your paint gets on your opponent then they're out." Loki said through a yawn.

Val stared at Loki as he spoke. Eyes burning his hatred into the slimy snake man. Loki stood with one hand in his pocket and another covering his yawning mouth. He was the picture of arrogance.

"I think my clan will be the raiders." Thor boomed, losing the seriousness he had donned for his part in the briefing.

"If that's what you want it'll make it easy for my clan to win." Loki sneered, removing his hand from his face and curling his upper lip at the hulking lightning man.

"Fat oafs like you drown in water don't they?"

Freya smiled awkwardly and Bragi placed his hand on his forehead. Val could see him say something and from reading his lips was sure he made out: "For the love of All Father, not again."

"They won't need to swim to crush your puny clan." Thor pouted, placing his hands on his hips.

"I bet they can't even sail." Loki retorted, like a child throwing a tantrum, moving a step closer to Thor.

The class had never seen either of them like this before. It was equal parts amusing and pathetic, or so Val thought.

Bragi began pacing in the background, shaking his head. Visibly becoming more annoyed with each passing remark. He got more agitated as the argument went on until he screamed:

"If you two don't cease this charade I will hold both of you underwater until the bubbles stop!"

The two bickering Gods went silent. Both of them looked taken aback, like scolded children. The class also went silent, they were shocked as Bragi was always so calm and nice, but also incredibly amused.

"I didn't know he was their mum." Alex whispered through a snigger.

Freya stepped forward and spoke to ease the tension and bring everyone back on task.

"Ok class please choose your weapons and the defending team get on the boat so you can set up. Raider team, you stay here and do the same." She said cheerily and carefree in the face of the strange argument that they had all just witnessed.

The defence team boarded the boat as it was sailed to the other side of the sprawling lake, out of sight of the castle docks. The boat sailed around a small inlet and the battle ground came into view. It was a small island with large stone walls and an open archway which lead to an even smaller village of wooden huts with thatch roofs.

The huts stood in a circle with a kind of town square set up in the middle. Surrounding this battle town was a huge arena. Large towers and viewing stands loomed overhead. They were tall and already filled with the boisterous spectators. In front of the jagged stone walls was a small beach, a landing area for the raiders.

The longboat pulled up to the beach and the team wordlessly disembarked, divided, with nervous eyes darting around, imitating the prey they were about to be.

"Everyone, come here a minute." Alice said shakily, as she slid on the sand.

The clans looked sheepishly at Alice, giving her their attention.

"Val has a plan that might just give us the upper hand." She said, turning to look at him.

Val was nervous. He hated public speaking and with his social status currently rock bottom he felt sick. He looked at the scared faces but all he saw was contempt. He briefly closed his eyes and tried to calm himself. He was determined to win back the favour of his peers. A quite resolve crept into him. He opened his eyes and told them his plan.

Chapter 12

RAID BATTLE

The defence team had taken their positions. Their weapons were dripping with paint and their brows with the nervous glisten of sweat. Val stood alone in the archway that was the only entrance into the replica town. He had no visible weapon and held a large circular shield in each hand. The shield in his left hand was green and sported the wolf symbol of Loki clan. In his right hand was a purple shield adorned with the lute sigil of Bragi clan.

From somewhere above a deep bellow sounded from a horn, signalling the beginning of his war.

A piercing wind struck Val's tight cheeks and clenched jaw. A deafening silence surrounded him. He could hear his heart thudding fast. His anxiety had faded. He made a conscious effort to control his breathing and he was calm. He had faith in the plan he and his friends had concocted.

He pushed the gaze of the audience out of his mind, for now there was only him. He stood alone at the precipice and he would win glory and the support of his peers. Most of all, he would prove to Kassandra that he wasn't as weak as the world wanted him to be.

From across the slithering water a single longboat appeared. Val knew what he had to do. He had gone over his plan in his mind thousands of times the previous night and he was ready. As the boat sailed onwards he remembered the advice Alex had given him. He reflected on the layout of the battlefield Alice had drawn for him.

'Strategy and cunning'. That was the advice Loki had given and despite his hatred for the man, it was advice he was ready to take.

The longboat drew near and Val could make out the burly ogre that was Erik Erikson stood on the bow. Just as Val had hoped he would. One last time he recalled Alex's advice. He took a deep breath and bellowed.

"Erik! You're weak and spineless. I bet you can't get a drop of paint on me."

Alex had told Val exactly what to say to entice Erik:

"Insult his strength and challenge him directly. He's proud and arrogant. I'm sure he'll come straight for you and the rest of his clan are sure to follow him."

The plan was commenced.

"As soon as this boat lands I'll kill you!" Erik shouted back, face red and axe raised in the air.

Erik had chosen not to bring a shield. Instead he had two axes, one was on his belt whilst his free hand held onto the sail ropes, steading him on the bow. The other was raised up in his hand. He imagined the steel was glinting menacingly in the sun, though, of course, it wasn't because it was made of black rubber.

The longboat was now close enough that Val, could make out the girls of Freya clan stood at the back. The ones he could see all had bows and in unison, they raised them. These girls had traded their makeup for war paint. One of them screamed:

"Fire!"

And a volley of rubber arrows arched through the sky straight at Val.

Val had predicted this tactic and he was ready for it. He raised his two shields and crouched down behind them, hiding his entire body. His arms braced as the thud of arrows struck his shields and fell lamely to the ground. He lifted his head to survey the area just in time to see Erik leap from the bow of the longboat and begin sprinting towards him. Both raiding clans were hot on his heels.

"Here comes the hard part." Val shuddered, peering over the top of his shields.

Erik was built for athleticism and he thundered towards Val like a lion stalking a gazelle. Now was the time. Val dropped his shields, turned and ran with all of his might towards the village.

"Don't look back. Don't look back. Don't look back." He repeated in his head as his burning lungs struggled to keep pace with his best effort at fleeing.

Erik was gaining ground fast. Val hadn't looked behind him, but he knew he was closing in. Val could not lose this race. If Erik caught him it would all be over. The hard, dirt ground sent dull aches into his knee joints as each step became heavier and heavier. He could feel the intense pain of cold air flooding his lungs with each breath.

Val was no athlete. He'd always sucked at football, even though he loved to play. He hated cardio and in the modern world he'd been stolen from, survival of the fittest had changed all meaning. However, the realm of the Gods was a harsh, literal world. Strength and ability was the biggest factor in your chances of survival.

Val was nearing the finish line. He could here Erik's elated, bloodthirsty screams close behind him. Erik was made for this world. Val summoned up the last of his fading strength for a final push. He ran straight towards the thatch hut at the edge of the town square and dived though a glassless window into it.

Erik smiled. His prey had just trapped itself and he was going in for the kill. He raced towards the hut, his entire raiding party close behind.

"Now!" Alice screamed.

Val breathlessly pushed himself off of the floor into a sitting position and looked out of the hole he had just dived through. Erik and his raiding party had stopped running and Val could see the look of confusion he was hoping for.

The entire defence team lined the roofs of the thatch huts that encircled the trapped raiders. Val heard the crack of drawstrings and arrows rained down on the square like a hailing death. Green and purple paint flew as the rubber arrows pelted their targets. One by one the raiders fell. Winded by the force, splattered with the paint of defeat. There were none left standing.

Alex dropped down from the roof above Val and offered him his hand. Val stepped through the hole and Alex raised Val's hand triumphantly. A booming roar filled the air. The crowd were on their feet. They stamped and clapped and cheered for the victorious defence team.

The raiders began to get up from the ground, skulking to the side of the square. Their heads were hung low, eyes averted. Val took in a deep breath, ready to let out his very own Viking victory cheer.

"I'm not done."

Erik pushed a boy from his clan off of himself and stood up, smirking.

"There's no paint on me yet Val." He said, sneering at Val.

The defence team archers drew their bows. They encircled Erik. They had the high ground. Their arrows were nocked. There was nowhere he could run.

"I challenge you to single combat!" Erik declared, raising his rubber axe and swinging it down to point at Val.

Val's eyes widened. The crowd fell silent.

Earlier in the year the students had learnt about this Norse custom in history class. It is seen as dishonourable and cowardly to decline a challenge of single combat. Erik had grasped control from Val with one sentence. If Val declined then their victory would be smeared. If anything he'd lose respect. All the effort and work he had put into his plan and now this?

There was only one option. Val sighed and wiped the sweat from his brow.

"I accept." He replied, looking up to face Erik head on.

Stepping out from behind one of the huts All Father made his way into the centre of the town. He walked towards Val and Erik.

"It has been declared that single combat will decide this battle!" All Father shouted for the crowds benefit. They were deafly silent, straining to listen and not wanting to miss any of the action.

"The terms are simple. You may use any weapon on this battlefield. If you leave the enclosure of the huts you forfeit. Winner takes all." All Father said. He ushered the remaining raiders out of the circle.

Alex shook Val's hand solemnly and then climbed back onto his perch of a thatch roof. As much as he believed in his friend, he knew it was over. Erik, for all his flaws, was a strong fighter. That was the entire reason they had come up with the ambush plan in the first place.

Val and Erik were left alone in the circle. They stared at each other. Val was expressionless but Erik smiled, knowing he had won.

"It doesn't look like you have a weapon. Don't worry, I'll make this even and pummel you instead." Erik boasted dropping his raised axe onto the ground and releasing the one on his belt as well.

Val remained silent, hands by his side. Erik raised his hammy fists and walked towards Val grinning the whole time. Val just stood there, waiting. Val had no chance against Erik in a fist fight. He'd lost every match he'd ever had with Erik and been knocked out cold more than once.

He was forlorn.

The crowd watched silently. They already knew the outcome but they were entranced. Its amazing how quickly a crowd of normal people can become so bloodthirsty. They wanted action and they wanted it now.

Erik continued forward slowly, ever the showman. He stepped towards Val and pulled back his hand for the knockout blow.

"You were too cocky." Val said, grinning.

"I win."

Erik lowered his fist and stepped back. The crowd strained to listen to what was being said. All Father raised an eyebrow, equally enthralled.

"Look at your top." Val said coolly, glancing down at Erik's polo.

Erik, All Father and the other onlookers all looked together as one. There was a small blob of green paint on Erik's clothing, right below where his bellybutton would be. Erik's mouth gawked open, he looked up at Val slowly and saw a small, dripping dagger in Val's right hand.

He had lost.

Chapter 13

TRANSGRESSIONS AND CONFESSIONS

The crowd looked on in stunned silence as Erik stood, jaw ajar, trying to comprehend what had just happened. Alex dropped down from the roof once more and stood at Val's shoulder.

"Did you like my gift then?" He said to Val quietly.

Just before the single combat match had begun, Alex shook Val's hand. It was then that he slipped him the dagger he had stashed before the raid battle. Val had palmed it and placed all of his faith in this single chance Alex had given him. His trust in his friend had paid off.

"That doesn't count." Erik said in disbelief, backing away slowly.

"This was a fist fight, it's against the rules."

Some of Thor clan murmured and nodded in agreement. Many of the other spectators began to wonder if this was true. It did seem dishonourable when Erik had thrown his axe's aside. Was it dishonourable?

"No young Erik." All Father said calmly, returning to the circular town square.

"The rules state that if a foe's weapon touches you and paint gets on you or your clothes then you are out." All Father said loud enough for everyone to hear.

Erik looked at All Father scathingly. He then began looking around for someone, anyone to back him up. There was no one.

"Val is the winner of this fight. The defence team win!" All Father yelled.

There was a moments pause as Val stood in front of Erik with a smile on his face. Then the arena erupted in deafening cheers, their doubts had vanished. The defence team started to get down from the huts, Alice first among them. She ran towards Val and Alex and embraced both of them.

"That was incredible." She said softly, burying her face in between them.

The rest of the team jogged and ran towards Val as well. They grabbed at him, patted him on the back congratulated him. Dean whispered to a few of the boys from Bragi clan and shot Val a cheeky smile. Dean, Simon and the other boys walked over to Val. Each grabbing a limb, they hoisted him off his feet and began tossing him in the air. They cheered amidst the backdrop of the paint covered replica town and at long last, Val too let out his victory scream.

The battle was over, the day was won and pretty soon everyone had boarded the longboats and returned to the castle. Val and the rest of Loki clan class one returned to their residence. They were elated, the first real victory the clan had had. Even the girls, who had never really spoken to Val, were smiling and congratulating him.

Dean tried his luck with Courtney and leant in for a kiss. He was hoping that the elation of their victory would smooth things over and make her give him a shot. She looked at him, eyes wide as his puckered lips made contact with her closed mouth. Ellie stepped in, dragging Courtney away as she threw a fierce slap at Dean, leaving a red hand print on his cheek.

Everyone bathed and changed their grimy clothes with speed. On the boat ride back Thor had told them there would be a celebratory feast in the hall. Despite being the leader of one of the losing clans, he seemed genuinely happy for defence team. He had even told them he would sneak them red mead, which he playfully mentioned was a lot stronger than the honey mead they were used to.

Having changed and washed, Val met with Alex and Alice. He was wearing the replica *Leeds United* shirt that Alex had gifted him for yule and the vegvisir necklace Alice had given him. The three walked down the corridor grinning ear to ear. They could already hear the cheers and excitement from the hall. It was all a little overwhelming.

They entered the hall and saw that the table layout had changed. There was now a head table in front of the throne and the Bragi clan from the defence team was already sat on it.

"Here he is!" A loud upperclassman shouted from within the hall.

He was referring to Val. Loki clan stood up from their table, clapping and cheering. Val had never had this much positive attention in his life. It was an amazing feeling. The trio took their seats on the newly positioned table. It was the winner's table, but to Val it was a throne of redemption. It seemed that everyone had forgotten the glory he had lost. He'd gone from social pariah to clan hero in minutes.

His plan had worked.

The celebrations got underway and Alex gorged on meats, breads and anything else that was within arm's reach. Thor came over to the table and, as he had promised, he poured them each a large tankard of red mead. Val took a sip and realised it tasted like berries. It was sweet to the tongue but harsh on the throat and it burned something fierce. Alice seemed to be enjoying it though, she gulped the strong drink like a pro.

Dean also seemed to like the mead – as if he needed more of a reason to be a loudmouth. He jumped onto the winners table and shouted, slurring a little:

"Three cheers for the victors." Students cheered a 'hip hip hooray' and Val was happy for the first time in weeks.

He looked around the hall, scanning it for Kassandra. As usual the clan tables weren't really mixing so he assumed she would be on the Freya table. He looked up and down but she was nowhere to be found. A sad pang twinged in him. He didn't know what he was expecting. It's not like their eyes were going to meet across the crowded room like one of those romance films his mum used to watch. Still though, her not being there brought down Val's mood.

Now he thought about it he didn't see her on the battle field either. Then again he had been so preoccupied with Erik he probably just hadn't looked for her.

He decided he needed some air so he quietly slipped away and left the hall through the raven doors. It was now the evening and the setting sun projected a deep orange mirror across the still lake. Hands in pockets, he began to mooch towards the lake. He heard a long creaking sound.

"I swear you are utterly an hedonic." A familiar teasing voice chimed.

"What does that mean?" Val asked perking up slightly but still facing away.

"It means you can't enjoy anything." Alice explained as Val heard her clumsily step towards him.

"It's her again isn't it?" Alice sighed.

Val nodded sadly and Alice moved in and hugged him tightly from behind. Her warm breath danced on his neck's short hairs. He lifted his arms and lightly grabbed her wrists. It was comforting to be held like this.

"You shouldn't let another person determine your happiness you know, it's not good for you." She said lightly. Val heard a slight twinge in her voice and felt more like he was intruding on her own internal monologue, than like he was being offered advice by a friend.

He felt the slight pressure of her chin on his shoulder and she pulled him tighter leant on him. He turned his head to look at her and saw a sad glisten in her tired eyes. Their gaze met and she smiled, but only with her mouth. Their faces were almost in touching distance and he could smell the sweet berry mead on her breath.

He could feel the warmth of her body, her soft bosom pressed tightly against his back. He blinked and their lips met. It was a delicate kiss, barely a kiss at all really. More an accidental touching of lips he thought. He opened his eyes and saw that hers were closed. She moved her mouth further into his and parted her lips. This was now a real kiss.

His fist kiss.

He parted his lips, allowing Alice to take over and get her wish, if just for a moment, but it felt wrong. He pulled away and she opened her eyes and stopped hugging him. She played with her fingers and his facial expression told her all she needed to know.

"I'm sorry." Alice said quickly, looking at the ground.

"I don't know what came over me."

"It must be the mead, it's strong stuff isn't it." Val said scratching the back of his head.

He knew it wasn't the mead but he wanted to give Alice an out. He valued her friendship and didn't want things to be awkward between them.

"Yeah." Alice said solemnly, still avoiding his gaze.

"Who knew I was such a light weight." She forced a laugh that faded quickly.

"Anyway I should probably be getting back to the party." She said, she turned and started to walk back towards the raven doors.

She stopped just shy of the entrance and without turning around said:

"She doesn't know what she's missing Val. She'd be lucky to have you." Then she slipped through the door and disappeared into the rowdy crowd.

The door of the golden raven closed behind her and the noise from the celebrations dulled. Val just stood there. He hadn't really seen Alice as a woman since the first time they met. Back then he thought she was cute but they'd become such good friends that he'd forgotten about that. He saw her as 'one of the guys', a good friend who he saw every day.

Had that changed now? After all she'd just given him his first kiss. More confusingly, he enjoyed it. Val pushed this thought to the back of his mind. This was Alice he was talking about. Alice who was so uptight, who scolded him for breaking rules and not taking classes seriously. Alice who spent all of her time with boys and barely spoke to the girls she roomed with.

Besides, he like Kassandra.

He shook his head and slapped his face with both hands. Alice was his friend and that was that. His mind was made up and he planned never to speak of this moment to anyone. Least of all Kassandra. If she ever actually talked to him again. Ever since that night she'd been avoiding him. He'd barely seen her around and the glimpses he did see of her were obscured by her band of Freya followers.

He put his hands back in his pockets and returned to the party.

There was now music playing, presumably some of Bragi clan. Tables were askew and students were dancing and chatting. It was lively and the atmosphere was energetic. From out of the crowd Alex appeared with a tankard in his hand and his belt fastened around his head like a bandana.

"Where have you been!" He slurred, swaying slightly.

"Our victory party is epic."

He stumbled next to Val and put his arm around him. His shirt was wet and he stunk of the sweet berry mead. He started walking off and turned around pointing his finger at Val and bobbing to the music as he moved backwards into the crowd.

Val laughed a little and began moving through the crowd back towards his table. Maybe some more mead would cheer him up. He wanted to enjoy himself more, this was his victory after all. It was just hard. He passed the now verry crooked, Loki table. Older clansmen were gathered around it and stood atop was Dean. He was shouting a call and response and the clan were responding, loving it.

"When I say Erik, you say sucks!"

"Erik"

"Sucks!"

"Erik"

"Sucks!"

Val couldn't help but grin at this – though it wasn't the most innovative chant.

Erik had been so awful to him for no reason and it was nice to see the tables turn. He stood watching the insulting chorus and saw Alex clamber onto the table from the other side. He watched as Alex put his arm around Dean and raised his tankard up high. Alex joined in with the chorus loudly.

Val had never heard his voice raised before. He always spoke so quietly. This was definitely going to be a memorable night.

The music stopped suddenly and the chatter died down. Val noticed people turning to the top of the hall and he followed their gaze. All Father was stood in front of his throne, he did not look pleased.

Everyone was now silent having noticed All Father and they were watching him in anticipation.

"When I say Erik, you say sucks!"

Alex and Dean chanted loudly, not realising that the rest of the room was now silent. They both turned around, noticing that their clan were no longer joining in. They both stopped when they met All Father's stern gaze.

Two deer in high beam headlights.

"You will all go to bed now." All Father said through gritted teeth.

"The celebrations are over."

All Father turned towards a very sheepish looking Thor. He had his head bowed, his shoulders were crunched inwardly and he was twiddling his two forefingers. For such a large man, he looked three feet tall in front of All Father's almighty, one eyed, gaze.

"I'll deal with you later." He said sternly, shooting an angry glace at the bumbling giant.

He turned back to face the students, some of whom were swaying involuntarily. Wordlessly he pointed towards the door, shaking his head and everyone made a mad dash to clear the hall, Val included.

Swept along by his clan, Val was almost carried back to the shield door and his common area. He saw Alice, also caught up in the wave of drunk, rushing students. Her eyes met his for just a second, then she looked away quickly and disappeared into her room. In turn Val went into his, he looked out of the window and saw the strange flicker of the light again.

He shook his head and brushed it out of his mind. He got under his bed furs hoping that things between him and Alice would be more normal in the morning.

Chapter 14

SWEET SIXTEEN

Val was scared. He didn't know why but the cold grip of fear was suffocating him. He felt like he was moving. He tried to flex his legs but he couldn't feel them, the same went for his arms. In fact, other than the odd feeling of motion, he couldn't feel anything. His mind was awake but his body was asleep, an unwilling passenger.

The area was shrouded in darkness. He couldn't see a thing, couldn't even make out shapes like a person usually can when it's dark. He wondered if his eyes were closed. It's a strange thing to not be aware of, the position of your eyelids, but when you can't feel anything at all it's possible that they could be closed without you knowing.

He strained and the screens of darkness started lifting, like a castle drawbridge. Little by little the light started to seep in. With tremendous effort, Val had opened the blinds.

The light was dim. Having his eyes open wasn't much better than leaving them closed but he was now beginning to see shapes as he got used to the dim lighting. The walls looked cave like. They were jagged and seemed to be made of dirt, maybe a tunnel underground?

There were unevenly spaced torches bolted to the wall, their flames flickering as if a slight breeze was coming from up the tunnel. Val couldn't feel the breeze though, he still couldn't feel anything.

He realised that his eyeline was way higher up than usual and that he was looking downwards and moving backwards. He couldn't move his head but he did manage to move his pupils to the edge of his eye socket. He saw unfamiliar legs facing away from him. He realised he was being carried by someone, but who and where were they taking him?

As Val's floating body was carried further down the tunnel, it started to widen and the tunnel had more structure. There were now wooden beams sticking into the ground and shooting up to the roof. There were planks of wood lining the wall and more torches, making it easier to see. Val almost wished it wasn't easier to see though.

There were small cramped cages piled on top of each other. Each cage had a motionless person inside. Somehow Val knew they were alive. Maybe they had the same issue as he did and couldn't feel or move their bodies? He made out the figure of a boy, laid lifeless within the cage. Lifeless, apart from his eyes which were open and following him as he was carried further in.

After being manoeuvred a little further, Val saw an empty cage. The only empty cage of the many he had seen. This cage was a little bigger than the others and had nothing stacked on top. It also had shackles, the sight of which made Val's heart pound even more. It's a strange feeling when your body is numb because you can still feel your heartbeat In exactly the same way you always could. However, because the heart beat is all you can feel, it's overwhelming. The beating war drum of your own terror. Internal and everlasting. It's dull thud filling your ears and reverberating around your skull. Like a score from a horror film that's entirely yours.

Val's body was violently swung around so he could no longer see the cage. He looked to the top of his vision and saw a shadow of a girl being carried by a hooded figure.

The girl had lifeless arms and looked like a corpse. Val realised she was looking at him from the top of her eyes, as her head was lolling over the cloaked figure's shoulder. The figure took a step away, further into the light of a mounted torch. Val was horrified.

It was Kassandra!

What was she doing here?

He tried to call out to her but his mouth was numb and unmoving, he couldn't form the words. The cloaked figured knelt down and propped Kassandra up against the back of a cage. Her lolling head swaying on her breast, her eyes still looking straight at him. The glint of her deep blue iris told him she was still alive.

She had to be alive.

Val had to find a way to escape and save her.

He realised that he too had been propped up in a cage. His captor was also cloaked and Val could not see his face. The cloaked figure and Val's captor both turned away from their respective cages at the same time and walked towards each other. Meeting in the middle, the two became one figure and walked back the way they had come.

Val was confused. How had the two cloaked figures moulded into one?

Was this some kind of Norse magic? Seidr, he recalled All Father calling it before. He looked back at Kassandra and her eyes met his once again. He needed to reassure her, let her know he was alive, but how?

Val couldn't move his body, let alone speak.

"Think Val, think!" He willed himself to come up with something. Then it hit him, his eyes.

He could move his eyes.

He'd managed to open them earlier, even if they were a heavy castle drawbridge. He could to it again. He mustered his will power and winked, in slow motion, with his left eye.

At the same exact time, Kassandra winked with her right eye. Maybe she had the same idea? It was a little eerie that they had both winked at the same time though. It wasn't natural. Just like when the two cloaked figures became one. Val heard steps. One of the cloaked figured walked past his cage. As he reached the cage he split into two, then turned back into one as he continued along the path to the part of the cave Val hadn't seen.

What was going on?

The eyes blinking in time, the two cloaked figure being so in sync. Them becoming one in the middle then slipping apart again when walking past this particular cage.

Then it dawned on him.

There was no other cage, it was a mirror.

That made sense, a mirror would explain how two people could become one when walking into the middle and how one person could become two but only when walking past.

How could he have been so stupid. It's amazing how much your mind can struggle in the dark.

But what about Kassandra. Val had never seen himself in the mirror, only Kassandra. How does that work? Unless he was Kassandra, or seeing through her eyes.

No, that couldn't be it, how could he move her eyes?

Val's vision began to blur and darkness set in again. With a huge breath Val sat bolt upright and opened his eyes. He was in the boys room and the dim light of sunrise was streaming through the curtainless window. He looked down and could see his own body. He stretched his arms out in front of him, relieved that he could move them.

Was it just a dream?

It could have been. That would be the logical answer, but it was so vivid. Val couldn't shake the idea that it was something more. He looked at his outstretched hands and saw they were trembling. He realised that he was still awash with fear from the dream. He needed to tell someone. All Father perhaps?

He gingerly got out of bed and dressed quietly. His clothes felt disgusting against his slimy skin. He was drenched in cold sweat. He struggled to pull a sock on and then threw it aside and decided to stick his bare, wet foot into his boot to save time.

Alex was snoring loudly in the bed next to his. He never snored, perhaps it's the after effects of the mead? Dean was laid starfish on the bed, on top of the furs with one leg bent and trailing on the floor. Simon wasn't even on his bed. He was on the floor, sat slightly with his head and arms lolling onto the bed whilst his lower body, positioned like a contortionist on the floor.

They were all obviously feeling the effect of Thor's mead and weren't going to be any help to Val. On the bright side, it wasn't technically dark outside right now so he shouldn't be breaking any rules by sneaking out.

Val crept through the bedroom door and out of the shield door. He walked slowly down the corridor, trying to control his steps, make them light so he wouldn't create that annoying echo sound that boots makes on stone when its quiet.

He opened the door into the hall and approached All Father's throne. He grabbed the front of the seat cushion and pulled it upwards, causing the throne to tilt. He heard that all too familiar crack and saw the passage with the stairs open up in front of him. He hurried down and walked quickly to All Father's chamber. He marched straight into the blue teleportation light, completely unafraid this time.

Once again he was confronted by the golden desk and curious ravens on their perch.

He approached the desk apprehensively and saw a half written parchment sitting askew and facing away from him. He heard a creaking noise and looked up to see the one-eyed God opening the painting door to the right hand side, behind the desk.

"What brings you to my chamber again young Val?" All Father asked, smiling. He had obviously quelled his rage from the previous night when he discovered his students were drunk and rambunctious.

Val looked at All Father and before he could stop himself he rattled through the contents of his vivid dream. He recanted the tunnel, the cages with people locked up inside, the fact that he couldn't move and was being carried by a hooded figure. He ended the tale with his realisation that he was looking in a mirror and he was Kassandra.

All Father stood still, listening patiently to what must have seemed like the ramblings a child tells their parents after a bad dream. He lifted his hand to his beard and stroked it thoughtfully. His eyes flickered, but only for a moment. He then slowly and with deliberate action, pulled his chair back with one hand. He left just enough room to sit down unencumbered by the desk's lip. He leant forward clasping both hands together with elbows bent, propped up on the golden shimmer of the desk.

"Thank you for coming to me with this Val. I will look into it." He said dryly, not looking Val in the eyes.

"Do you think I was seeing through her eyes sir?" Val asked, knowing it sounded mad.

"Who can say?" All Father replied, unmoving.

"I know you have many questions but I don't have the answers. Please carry on as normal and I will look into this and check on Miss Johnson's wellbeing."

Val opened his mouth as if to speak. He had so many questions. For some reason he could tell that this wasn't the time. He closed his gaping mouth and turned around to leave. He felt defeated. He was no closer to an answer and some kind of sixth sense told him that All Father knew more than he was letting on.

Frustrated, Val walked out of the chamber, closing the door behind him. He turned slightly when closing the door and saw Freya stood behind it. She raised her finger to her lip, telling him not to say anything.

Once the door was closed she took Val's wrist and lead him out of the passage.

Her grip was warm and tender, yet tight enough that she could almost drag him with her surprising strength. She lead him out of the hall and took the door to the left, the opposite one to where Val's clan was located. She led him down a side passage along the corridor and stopped. She looked around anxiously then suddenly grabbed both of Val's shoulders and pushed him against the wall, her face inches from his.

"I might be able to help you." She said in a hurried whisper.

Her breath was warm and smelt like honey mead, it wasn't a bad smell. Being this close to Val, he could see just how delicately beautiful her face was. She had two little dimples in her cheeks and her lips were thick, but not like the thickness associated with lip filler back in his world.

"If I do help, you can't tell any of the other Gods about this ok?" She said softly, caringly even.

Val nodded and she silently took him by the hand and lead him further down the passageway. Her hands were soft and her skin had a slight spring to it. She lead Val to a small door and, looking around one last time, she opened it and ushered him inside.

Val looked around and saw a modest chamber with a familiar set up. On the back wall was a medium sized oak desk, there was a door to the right hand side behind it. This room had more furs and throws than the other God's chambers. You could have laid almost anywhere on the floor and never felt the cold stone.

Freya beckoned to Val to take a seat on a fur laden sofa. He did and she sat closely next to him. It was a little uncomfortable being this close to her. Her gorgeous femininity intimidated Val a little, but her kind presence eased his anxiety. She placed both of her hands on his leg and leaned in close and he told her everything.

Freya was a good, active listener. She nodded in the right places, replied when needed and watched Val's lips with intense purpose. You could see why she taught a seduction class, she knew how to make a man feel important. She could put you at ease whilst still oozing sexual tension and she knew it. Val didn't mind though. After All Father brushed him off it was nice to feel heard and listened to.

Freya let Val talk until his story was finished and then she leaned back thoughtfully.

"Have you ever heard of Seers?" She asked quietly.

"No, I don't think so?" Val replied, shuffling further along the couch.

"Seers number in the few Val. It's a rare ability. The ability to see into the future, make prophesies or, in some cases, see through the eyes of one you have a strong connection with." She said wistfully, placing her arm softly on the back of the sofa.

Val looked at Freya who was sat up straight and showing off all of her natural curves.

"So, do you think I really did see through Kassandra's eyes?" Val asked, pulling his arms in close and hugging himself.

"Who can say, but if you did it's very worrying. She's one of my favourite clanswomen after all." Freya smiled, turning to look at Val.

She placed her hand on his knee once again and he prayed not to blush. The warmth from her touch spread slowly up his thigh and he felt simultaneously at ease and ridged as a longboat's hull.

"Seers are a contentious subject in this world Val." She said smoothly, dipping her head and looking up at him.

"Please keep this conversation between us and I will try and do some digging on the matter."

Val agreed and realised that Freya was now speaking a lot more like her students did. The Gods normally had a strange way of saying things but this had all but left Freya now. Val was impressed, she'd managed to pick up speech patterns from the students and use them herself.

"Oh and Val, there won't be any classes today to let the students rest up after the party." Freya said, standing up from the sofa and opening the door for Val.

Freya bid Val goodbye and he left her chambers and headed back to Loki clan's residence. He had more questions than answers but it was comforting to know someone believed him and took his dream seriously.

As he walked down the corridor he saw a clock which said: 'April first' above the ticking hands. Val let out a single, callous laugh as he realised that today was his birthday.

"Typical." He thought.

Chapter 15

SUSPECTS

Val returned to his clan's common area and slumped, exhaustedly into one of the green, leather armchairs. The heat from the fire was welcome after the morning he had had. His mind was racing amid flashbacks to the dream and a dull headache that thumped on his frontal cortex.

After a little while the sun was shining high in the sky and streaming in through the skylights in the common area. Clansmen started waking and passing through the room. None of them really spoke, but some let out groans as they shuffled past Val, zombie like, and headed for breakfast.

Alex exited the bedroom looking rough. His hair was a mess, his eyes were shadowed and the lacklustre expression on his face was enough to warn anyone about the effects of drinking. He half sat, half fell into the chair next to Val.

"You're up early." He mumbled, eyes glazed.

"I've been up for a while, I need to tell you something but by the look of you it should probably wait for later." Val said, still sporting a thousand yard stare that was two parts sleep deprivation and one part traumatising nightmare.

Alice stumbled into the room, a line of equally unkempt girls behind her. The line splintered off, heading for breakfast as Alice moved over to her two friends. She sat in the chair opposite Val and looked away sheepishly when he met her gaze.

He had almost forgotten about their kiss from the previous night. In any other circumstance he would have felt awkward, but he was too trapped in his own mind to care. He looked at Alice and saw that her scarlet hair had formed ringlets in her sleep. Two stray strands had fallen over her right eye. It was a good look.

"Let's get you two something to eat. I need to talk to you both and I can't do it if you're hungover." He said frankly, rising from his seat as they groggily watched him.

They agreed and Val led them towards the hall. For a moment he swore he could see them floating, drawn towards the smell of bacon: the undisputed *Pied Piper* of the hungover.

They entered the hall. It was a dull morning as the students clutched their heads, held their queasy stomachs and regretted their existence to a backdrop of bacon and eggs.

Alex groggily grabbed at a plate stacked high with bacon medallions. Too lazy to use a fork he grabbed at the dark pink pieces and began shovelling them into his mouth. Usually he had a content look as he ate but today his eyes were hollow.

Alice, more delicately, grabbed some fried bread and placed a fired egg on top. She gracefully cut into this with a knife and fork and ate small bites, ensuring to include both egg and bread each time.

Val wasn't really interested in the food., gnawing on the same bacon medallion for the entire time the other two were eating.

"There's a Jotun!" Dean screamed running into the hall.

"There's a Jotun in the castle!"

The dishevelled students began rising, confused and scared. Val jumped to his feet, ready to run. They had learnt about Jotun in history class. The fearsome race of frost giants, hell bent on destroying the world of the Gods.

How could one have gotten into the castle?

Where did it even come from?

"April fools!" Dean yelled, doubling over and clutching his stomach with laughter.

Most of the students sat back down, shaking their heads. They were too ill to shout at him. One or two threw some fried bread at Dean in irritation.

"How is he not feeling as bad as we are?" Alice complained, returning to her breakfast masterpiece.

"Did he say April fools?" Alex asked, looking more alive than he had earlier on and raising his head.

"Isn't that your birthday?" He asked Val, stuffing another fistful of bacon into his mouth.

"Yeah." Val said quietly.

His birthday was of no consequence to him right now. He just wanted to tell them about his dream and what Freya had told him.

Val remembered last year telling Alex when his birthday was when they were getting to know each other. He made a joke about the day of April fools being his birthday, remarking at it being the world's way of telling him how his life would turn out. It was a well-rehearsed self-depreciation he had made annually back in their realm.

"Happy birthday." Alice smiled, though it was more of a grimace as she was still feeling less than ok.

"Thanks." Val said forcing a smile back at her.

After the two had finished eating and seemed to have perked up a bit, Val asked them to accompany him outside. He lead towards the quiet docks, knowing that no one would overhear them here as they'd all probably be heading back to bed. He took a seat on the edge of the dock, In the same place Kassandra had given him a glimpse of her upper leg as she put on her ice skates earlier that year.

That seemed like a lifetime ago now.

Carefully and without hesitation, Val told his friends everything. He recanted the dream, spoke of how he thought All Father was hiding something and told them about his personal chat with Freya. When he finished he continued staring across the glistening water. No one spoke for a little while. They probably didn't know what to say to him. Finally Alex breached the silence.

"I can't believe you got that close to Freya. I am so jealous." He said, dropping down next to Val on the edge of the dock. His added weight made the wooden planks creak.

The tension faded a bit and Val chuckled, feeling a bit more at ease. Alex had a knack of making him feel better with offhand jokes and comments. The boy simply didn't have a serious bone in his body.

"The people in cages. You don't think they're the missing students do you?" Alice asked quietly, crouching down behind them.

The thought had crossed Val's mind but he wasn't even sure what he'd seen was real.

"So you believe me then?" Val asked raising his head to meet his gazing friends.

"Of course we do mate." Alex said, lightly punching Val's shoulder.

Alice also sat down, forcing her way between them, her bare legs kicking through the air as she dropped them over the docks edge and leant back on her hands.

"The real question is, what do we do now?" Alex mused, placing his chin on his hands and staring into the glistening water.

"I think we should start in the archive and see what we can find out about these Seers." Alice said, always the wise woman of the group.

Val agreed, despite Alex's moans about reading study books when he was hungover. The three left the docks and headed to the archive. Alice took the lead as she was the only one that spent any time in there. She lead them to a large silver door with carvings of books and runes on it. Opening the door carefully, they entered.

The archive was a sprawling library of scrolls, tomes, texts and leather-bound books. It was a bibliophiles dream. There were bookshelves everywhere, they seemed to go on forever and they reached all the way to the tall ceiling. There were ladders with wheels on every case so people could reach the top shelves.

Alice lead them through a winding maze of texts until they reached a circular clearing in the middle of the forest of literature. Stood in the middle of the circle was a wooden spiral staircase with intricate carvings on its banisters. As they walked in short ascending circles, Val saw a small hole in the ceiling that would lead to the second floor. He stuck his head through and pulled himself up to find an attic setting.

The roof had rafters and there was limited lighting. There were a lot of bookcase here too but they were a lot smaller and looked old. There was a musty smell and most of the books he could see had a thick layer of dust covering them.

"They keep the older stuff up here." Alice said, pulling herself up through the hole.

"How are we going to find what we're looking for?" Alex asked, following behind her.

"I'll find it, you two just wait here." She winked playfully and disappeared amidst the non-fiction forest.

Alex found a wooden bench with a school desk attached and sunk himself into it. He folded his arms on the table and rested his head there. Val took a short lap around and found a long, thin pole that was attached to something on the roof. He played about with it and noticed that it moved forwards and backwards. He moved the pole and discovered that it was attached to a blind that was covering a skylight. A ray of light shone in, revealing a cyclone of swirling dust particles.

"Good job, it was too dark to read properly in here." Said a cheery Alice returning from the written maze.

She skipped over to Alex's desk, clearly loving having her friends in the archive with her. She dropped a large, leatherbound tomb in front of Alex, who sat up startled at the loud thud next to his head. Alice sniggered and leant over the tome blowing the top layer of a multi-layered dust armada , into Alex's face.

"Why?" Alex whined coughing and waving his arm to disperse the dust cloud.

Alice opened the tome to the index and used her forefinger to move down the list until she found what she was looking for.

"Here we are. Chapter 17, Seers and Prophecies." She said happily.

She thumbed through the tome's yellowing pages until she found the correct one and began reading aloud.

"The Seer was a position of great power in the realm of the Gods. Known for the ability to predict the future, glimpse the past, or in some rare cases, see through the eyes of others. Most Seers come from long lines of Seers and are trained in the art from a young age. There have been many famous prophesies through time but perhaps the most iconic was the Ragnarök prophesy." She read, carefully turning the delicate pages as she went.

"Ragnarök, isn't that what All Father said on our first day here?" Val asked, kneeling down beside her.

"This prophesy was told for All Father and it stated that he would adopt the son of a Jotun. This child would become the trickster God of assassination and one day rain down fire and ash upon the realm of Gods."

She stopped reading and the three looked at each other with shared realisation.

"Who does that remind you of?" Alex asked sarcastically, leaning back in his chair with his arms dangling.

"It's got to be Loki. It all makes sense." Val said through gritted teeth and clenched fists.

Loki had, after all, made Kassandra his servant as punishment for their date. He was disliked and shunned by the other Gods. Thor argued with him before the raid battle. Even All Father had less enthusiasm when explaining Loki's clan at the blood stone ceremony. To top it all off, the description matched him perfectly.

"What does it say next?" Val asked, grasping at the heavy tome to look for himself – not that he could read many runes yet.

"It doesn't, the next page has been ripped out." Alice replied, calmly closing the tome.

"Think he did it himself?" Alex asked, catching himself as he leaned back too far and nearly fell over.

Val did think this. It made sense. A tome that spelled out his evil deeds. What worried Val more was that this prophesy was delivered directly to All Father and yet he had allowed Loki to teach them. That's what the glint in his eye was when Val explained his dream. All Father knew it was Loki all along. That's why he kept telling them to 'leave it to him' and not to get involved. Val felt sick. Maybe this whole school was just a charade. A butcher's shop for Loki's twisted plans – whatever they might be.

"We have to stop him." Val said seething with rage as he stomped to his feet.

"Calm down." Alice said sharply, backing away from him.

"We need to think about this, we don't have all the information yet."

"She's right mate. I know you're angry and I don't like him either but we don't have any proof yet do we?" Alex said, returning his chair to an upright position and trying to calm Val down.

It wasn't working. Val's blood was running hot. He wanted revenge. He wanted to save Kassandra. He wanted it now.

"Ok fine. We'll get some proof then. Tonight we'll sneak into his chambers and see what we find." Val said, leaning over the table, putting his weight onto his palms.

"Are you sure this is a good idea?" Alice asked worriedly, hugging the dusty tome.

"It's as good as any and this is time critical." Val said, already moving to leave the archive.

Alice and Alex shared an exasperated glance. Val wasn't going to listen to reason. They followed him out of the archive, resigned to his whims.

Chapter 16

SLEUTHING

That night Val and the others waited until their roommates had fallen asleep and snuck into the common area to go over their plan. Loki's chamber was only down the corridor from their residence. The plan was simple, sneak in, look for evidence or a hidden entrance to the cave Val had dreamed about and get out.

Alice and Alex were less than thrilled about the idea of making an enemy out of Loki. Alice wasn't happy about the lack of evidence and was very vocal about this. However, Val dismissed her, certain that his gut feeling was right.

Alex was trying to play mediator and calm Val down. It was his preferred role in the group, despite his laidback ways he was always putting himself in the middle in the interest of harmony among his friends.

"Let's go." Val whispered, waving them to follow him as he stood up.

The three headed through the shield door and down the corridor to Loki's chambers. Carefully, Val felt behind the painting, just as Loki had done when he caught Val and Kassandra at the lake. His fingers found a latch and as quietly as he could, he undid it. The painting swung open and they stepped inside. Alex closed the entrance behind them.

"Ok, lets split up and look. I'll check his desk." Val commanded, striding over to the large desk.

Val moved behind the desk and started routing through draws. He found stacks of parchment in the first draw but nothing of note. In the second draw was a silver hilted dagger with a sharp curved point to the blade. It was a fierce looking weapon, despite being small.

He felt almost drawn to this weapon. It was strange, but it wasn't the reason he was here and he was no thief so he put it back where he found it and closed the draw.

"Found anything?" Val whispered, looking up from the draws.

Alex was looking at some shelves that hadn't been there last time Val was in the room. He turned to face Val and shook his head. Alice was stood in the corner, arms folded, staring at the large portrait of Loki behind Val.

"I don't like this." She said, standing still and tugging at her polo through her folded arms.

"We really shouldn't be in here."

"If you know that then why are you?" Said a scathing voice.

The trio looked around but there was no one there. Val felt something brush against his leg and jumped backwards, knocking the Loki portrait askew. A large, long haired, speckled cat strode past him. It jumped effortlessly onto the desk and sat down, licking it left paw.

"Where did that come from?" Alex said, turning his head erratically to find the source of the voice.

"Who are you calling a that?" The scathing voice said again.

The thee looked towards the voice which seemed to be coming from the cat. How could that be, cats can't talk.

Confused and on edge, Val moved around the desk until he, Alice and Alex were shoulder to shoulder, looking at the cat.

"What, have you never seen a talking cat before?" The cat said, raising its paw.

The trio looked at each other and then back at the cat.

"You can talk?" Alex said, mystified, mouth agape.

"No, I'm communicating with you telepathically." The cat said sarcastically.

"Yes I can talk you imbecile."

Val couldn't believe his eyes, or his ears.

A talking cat?

They'd all seen some strange things since coming to the realm of Gods but nothing like this. No one had prepared them for talking animals.

"Why are you here?" The cat asked, it's wide eyes staring at them.

"We got lost looking for the toilets." Alex said quickly, scratching the back of his head and averting his eyes.

"All three of you?" The cat said, looking at the two boys and girl who were stood in front of it.

"I can't believe members of the illustrious Loki clan can't think of a better lie." The cat said, shaking it's furry head.

The cat sighed and stood up, pacing back and forth along the desk. It's sharp claws clattered with every step. It was too large to be a normal house cat like the type they knew from their world. This cat was as big as a Staffordshire Bull Terrier, with long speckled silver fur. It's face was oddly large as well.

"Tell the truth. Why are you here?" The cat said once again eyeing each of them in turn.

"We're looking for Loki, we need to talk to him." Val offered, raising his hands outwards and showing open palms.

"Ah ok." The cat said, stopping at the edge of the desk and looking Val in the eyes.

"That must explain why you were searching through his draws. Obviously a God could quite easily fit in there. Perhaps, it's where he sleeps yes?" The cat said.

Val couldn't think of a way out of this. The cat was clever and they had been caught red handed.

"Ok, as much I'm enjoying that look on your faces, it' time for some real answers." The cat said jumping off the desk towards them.

Whilst in the air the cats legs started getting long and it's face started bubbling and changing. The three backed up, having no idea what was happening. They shared a look of confusion and Alice looked terrified. She had gone pale, even more so than usual.

The cat's paws landed on the floor, it had now morphed into a man; Loki.

He stood in front of the three of them with his signature sneering smirk plastered across his face.

"Are you ready to answer honestly now?" Loki asked threateningly, raising a fist just above stomach height as he moved towards Val.

"Exams are coming up soon and we were looking for the answers." Alice said, turning her face towards the floor and playing with her fingers awkwardly.

Val looked at her with quiet admiration. She had come up with the perfect lie. There was no way they could tell Loki that they suspected him of kidnapping students and that they knew he as the son of a Jotun.

"Was that so hard?" Loki sneered, seeming to believe the lie.

"I'd expect nothing less of my clan, sneaking around in the dark to steal answer to exams. If you'd have been more careful about it I might have even let you off. The problem is, that you're all so useless." He spat as he shook his head.

Loki moved closer to the three and paced across their line as he monologued.

"When All Father made me do this job for him I was expecting talented young minds I could mould into my replicas. However, I'm stuck with the likes of you three who couldn't sneak into a hall filled with your own copies. Do you have any idea how disheartening it is to have a group of rule breakers in my clan who keep getting caught? Do you think I want you to lose the glory competition? Now I'm going to have to reprimand you, but I'm the one really getting punished here. That blundering thunder oath is going to hold this over me when we lose to him and his pig headed clan." Loki finally took a breath, his eyes shooting daggers at them with each passing step.

He seemed disturbed, insane even. His verbalised thoughts were all over the place. It was concerning for Val who genuinely thought that he might get dragged away on the spot.

Loki stopped pacing. Turned away from them and sighed. He raised his hand loosely above his shoulder.

"Just leave." He sighed again, this time it was heavier and disheartened.

The trio turned to look at each other and Val started to move towards the entrance, glad for a chance to escape the lunatic. He backed away slowly, still staring at Loki's limp, arrogant hand. He turned and opened the portrait and the three of them skulked back to the common area silently.

They stepped over the lip of the shield door and let it close behind them. Val walked slowly into the common area and there was a figure sat in one of the green leather armchairs in darkness.

"You did it again didn't you." The familiar shadow said disappointingly.

The figure got up out of the chair and knelt down in front of the fire place, lighting it. A flickering light danced around the room lighting up the figure's face.

It was Simon.

"Winning a battle isn't going to be enough this time Val. Everyone's been trying so hard to raise us out of last place. It's the only goal I have right now." Simon said, rubbing his tired eyes.

"Well, did you get caught?" He asked, still facing away from the trio.

"Yeah." Val said sullenly.

Simon stood back up and without looking at them went back into the bedroom. Val moved towards the armchair with drooped arms and collapsed into it. He looked up at Alice who looked annoyed. Alex sat opposite him, hunched over.

"I told you this was a bad idea. Now everyone is going to hate us." Alice said, her eyes glistening but her face contorted.

Val reflected on the little bit they had learned in the chamber. Loki can transform into a cat. He's still a horrible person who seems to hate humans and takes pleasure in berating them.

"I know its him." Val said quietly, looking down to avoid her emotional eyes.

"I'm not so sure." Alice sighed, kneeling by the fire and facing away.

"I want to see it how you do Val but I'm just not sure it is him."

Val couldn't understand why she was saying this. It was obviously Loki. It just made sense, it all added up. How could she not see it? He was the one who had been kidnaping the students for months. It must be him. Val knew it deep in his gut that Loki was the kidnapper and now he'd taken Kassandra. It didn't matter what Alice said. He'd uncover this mystery and save her no matter what.

"I don't know mate. He's awful and I don't like him, but I don't know if he's the one behind these disappearances." Alex said quietly, standing behind Val's chair.

"Even you?" Val said looking up at his friend and feeling betrayed.

"You heard that monologue of his, he sounded genuinely upset that we were going to lose points. If he was kidnapping students then why would he care? If anything he'd want us creeping around at night so he could take us easier, right?" Alex reasoned, placing a hand on Val's shoulder.

He shrugged it off.

Alex was his best friend in this realm. He'd always stuck with him. He was the first one who wanted to help him when everyone was ignoring him before the raid battle. He always told Val to brush it off and think of a plan to turn things around. Why was he being like this?

Why couldn't he see what Val saw?

This was Loki's fault. He was always one step ahead of Val and now his friends didn't even believe him anymore.

"If that's how you feel then just stay out of my way." Val said icily as he stood up and turned towards the bedroom.

"Val, it's not like that. We just need some actual evidence." Alice said turning to look at him and reaching out with one limp hand as tears streamed down her face.

Val didn't care what she had to say, he didn't even care that she was crying. If they weren't with him then they were against him. He didn't need them anyway. He could save Kassandra on his own.

Without looking back, Val opened the bedroom door and crawled into bed. Alex followed behind him but Val refused to look at him and crunched into a ball, under the bed furs, he faced away from his once best friend.

The next day All Father made an appearance at breakfast. He gave a short announcement expressing his concern at students wandering the castle at night. He told them that this rule was for their safety and said that in these trying times where students had gone missing not too long ago, it was imperative that they follow the rules and allow the Gods to protect them.

Val thought he was full of hot air. All Father knew that Loki was behind this and he was so concerned with protecting his adopted frost giant son that he'd let the students be collateral damage.

The Loki clan table was quiet that morning. They had all heard the news that it was their clansmen who had broken this rule and them who would bear the brunt of the punishment. Their glory score had plummeted and they were back in last place. It was hard for a lot of them to take. They had tried so hard in the class one raid battle and it was all for nothing now.

The week dragged on and Val barely spoke a word to anyone. Alice and Alex were feeling the brunt of the Loki clan anger as it got out that they were involved with the rule breaking. Val didn't care. He had bigger problems now than social status.

Who cared if his foolish clan didn't like him anymore? They had all bought into this glory point system and the fake school they were attending. Val knew better now. They were all victims, just waiting to be plucked by Loki.

Throughout the week the other classes participated in their raid battles. Unfortunately, Loki class lost every one of them. Some of the older students were strong, but they were no match for Thor's upper clansmen who had been gifted superior genes for muscular development and a lust for fighting. That only made things worse as the mood surrounding Loki clan hit rock bottom.

Everyone was on edge, everyone blamed Val, Alice and Alex.

Erik had regained his confidence now his clan was firmly in the lead. In the classes he shared with Val's clan he took every opportunity to loudly boast at his clan's victories. Val tried to ignore him but the others couldn't. Especially Simon who was now actively avoiding Val. Simon had always been relatively quiet, he followed Dean around and said very little. Now, however, he was starting to be just as vocal as his friend. Unfortunately for Val, this was the worst time for him to find his voice.

Bragi, not sensing the tension, decided to try flyting again. As you might expect, it didn't go well. This time it was Simon versus a Thor boy called Kyle. He was one of Erik's new cronies and he was even more bone headed than his boss. He was as wide as he was tall, he would have made the perfect shield for Val back in the raid battle.

Unfortunately for Simon, he was also pretty stupid and quick to anger. When Simon said:

"You're fatter than a pig and wider than you are tall. You can barely speak a proper sentence, you neanderthal."

Kyle lost his head. His face turned a deep shade of purple and he charged at Simon. Bragi had to interject yet again, blocking a panic punch from Simon and restraining a writhing Kyle Angrily he told the class that he wouldn't be teaching them flyting anymore.

Chapter 17

LIVING OFF THE LAND

As spring became summer the clans changed back into their thin cloaks and summer trousers. Val had started to become a bit of a recluse. He barely spoke anymore and spent all of his free time sat alone on the docks.

Despite their little spat, his friends Alex and Alice still tried to talk to him at first. He didn't want to hear it though, he ignored their attempts and brushed them aside. Now, they seemed further apart than ever.

Val missed his friends, though he didn't like to admit it. It was lonely being by himself. He did, however, have a goal to keep him preoccupied: saving Kassandra. This was his obsession, his guiding light and it was fuelled by a deep hatred for Loki. Val hadn't snuck out since the night of the cat, but he was keeping a watchful eye on Loki during the day.

He was switched off during most classes, but during Loki's assassination class he was now the top student. He believed it would bring him closer to understanding Loki if he was good at the subject he taught. Besides, he was used to being unseen, always in the darkness.

After his victory over Erik in the raid battle and because he had been drawn to the beautiful silver hilted dagger in Loki's draw, the dagger was now Val's preferred weapon. Why fight a battle of strength when you can win with brains and tricks right?

He diligently took in everything the trickster God was trying to teach him, hoping to find something he could use against him. He learnt to stalk the shadows and make good use of his surroundings. All the while, never forgetting his goal.

During Thor's battle class Erik made a point of showing everyone that he was the superior fighter. He pummelled Val in every duel they had. Erik took a twisted pleasure in hurting Val and then announcing to the class just how great he was. His dutifully idiotic follower Kyle, would stand in Erik's corner and crow dim witted insults at Val as he took punch after punch. It was exhausting and humiliating, but no matter how hard he tried or how angry he got he just couldn't beat Erik in a fair fight.

Erik also took every opportunity to berate and publicly humiliate Val. He would bring up Loki clan being last, he would bring up Val being the main cause and he made fun of him for his beansprout physique. Not so long ago his reign of terror would have crushed Val, but now it all just seemed childish to him compared to the things he knew were going on behind the scenes. If anything it was just annoying, though the frequent trips to the healer's chamber provided a welcome break from the onslaught of classes.

It was sailing class Val struggled with the most. Njord was probably nicest to him out of everyone in the school right now. He complemented Val's now half decent sailing ability and was never anything less than a positive person. However, Val was so wrapped up in his own head that he barely even noticed this. He was fixated on Kassandra not being there. Knowing she was caged was eating him up inside and sailing class was the time he felt it the most as it was a class they had shared.

If ever there was a brief moment of respite where he forgot his dream, even for a second. A simple glace at the Freya girls would bring him crashing back down to earth. He frequently had flashbacks to the tunnels. He welcomed them, like an old friend. He wanted so desperately to gain a clue as to their whereabouts. Anything could help, so he leaned into the flashback dreams, but he turned up nothing.

The biggest issue for Val was how useless he felt. He wanted so badly to be able to save her, to at least find out where she was, but instead he was stuck playing the student. He was surrounded by people who either hadn't noticed or didn't even care that she was missing.

The girls from Freya clan who had followed her around seemed to have just carried on like nothing happened. Freya herself hadn't spoken to Val since telling him about seers. He was alone with the weight of her life on his shoulders, and as Erik loved to mention, he was only a weak beansprout.

Val actually tried to listen in Mimir's history lessons. It was the class that had first mentioned the Jotun and he was hoping for more information.

One day after class he stayed back, to Mimir's surprise. He asked the old God if he could tell him anything more about the Jotun. He specifically wanted to know if they had ever attacked humans. Unfortunately Mimir didn't know. He told Val that the Jotun had been wiped out a long time ago and much of the knowledge the realm once knew about them had been forgotten.

He told Val that it was illegal to even attempt to travel to Jotunheim these days, despite it being an uninhabited wasteland. Apparently there were concerns of powerful artifacts or bloody texts left there and All Father didn't want any of his people being corrupted or worse, bringing home some kind of plague.

Val was disappointed with the lack of new information, but he had learnt one thing that could be useful. The revelation of the Jotun being wiped out would mean Loki was the last one. Val had a horrifying thought that maybe Loki wanted to forcible mate with the students he had captured to create more half breed like himself. He quickly discredited his new twisted theory though when he realised that Tom was the first of the taken and he was a boy.

On one particularly warm day Loki clan was instructed to head into the forest where they had learnt archery in weapons week. The group of five girls and four boys, as Tom was still missing as well, trapsed inside.

The forest had a different atmosphere in summer. In winter it was pretty and full of snow and it stayed that way through most of spring. Now, however, the snow had gone and it was warm. There were insects buzzing around and the sounds of animals moving in the undergrowth. The trees and plants were various shades of green and they grew so close together you could get lost without even knowing it. In winter the tall trees were the only things with leaves and all the foliage was dead so it was easier to walk and navigate.

They arrived at the archery clearing, which now had no targets or bows. Instead there was a small hut that had been erected. Dean walked up cautiously and knocked on the hut. The door swung open and a sweet and familiar voice invited them inside. The group followed the voice and went inside the hut to find Freya sat behind a small desk. The hut was set up much like her classroom, with desks and benches for the students.

"Welcome to living off the land!" Freya said enthusiastically, opening her arms and standing at the front of the class.

"Since it's warm now All Father thought it would be a great idea to teach you some basic survival skills and who better to do the teaching than me, the God of hunting." She said in her familiarly bouncy tone.

Why was she acting like this?

She knew that Kassandra was missing, she knew and she'd promised Val she would fix it. Yet she was acting like nothing was amiss. Why was he the only one who cared. The only one not living in ignorant bliss in this school-setting nightmare.

Freya went on to tell them that living off the land was an important skill that would help them if they ever got lost in the forest or had to flee a warzone – not that there had been a war in hundreds of years in the realm of the Gods.

She started off by teaching them how to create fire 'the human way' as she called it. Basically, how to start a fire without magic. She lead them out into the forest and told them to collect different types of moss and wood. She asked them for kindling, which is small pieces of wood or moss that burns easily, this is basically natures lighter fluid. She also wanted medium thickness pieces of wood to act as the buffer and keep the fire going long enough to spread it to the thick pieces of wood, which she also wanted.

Once everyone had collected their ingredients, they sat in a circle facing Freya who explained to them how to create a miniature pyre. A pyre is normally used to burn a corpse and send the soul onto Valhalla, the Norse afterlife, but Freya assured them that it is also an easy way to start a fire by hand too.

You start by creating a circle with weighty rocks. Next you place your kindling in the middle. You then pile the medium sized pieces of wood facing upwards to form a triangle. Then you add the large pieces to the outside of the triangle, also facing up. Finally you use a piece of dry moss using one of the many fire lighting methods and add it to the centre pile of kindling. You lean in and blow lightly and soon it's all up in flames.

Val actually enjoyed this lesson. He found a subtle serenity in creating the pyre. It was easy to do, but kept his hands busy whilst his foggy brain thought about Kassandra. Once everyone's fires were pretty much burnt out, Freya took them all back to her new hut.

Whilst she was wrapping up the lecture a wild forest cat wandered in. Amid a chorus of "aww" from the girls, the large feline sauntered towards the head of the class. Freya bent down to pick it up but it hissed and decided to leave, pouncing carelessly back out the window.

The cat reminded Val of Loki. Quietly seething, he sunk lower into his seat at the back of the room. Whilst the clan was filtering out, Val decided it was a good time to ask Freya for any news. He waited for the other students to vacate the hut and then he walked to the front of the class.

"Have you got any news?" He whispered behind his hand.

Freya looked shocked, she probably wasn't expecting such a brazen approach. She had, after all, specifically told him to wait until she contacted him.

"Not really Val. I'm still digging into it. Just be patient for me, please." She pleaded with the angry boy, showing him her palms in a defensive way.

Val wanted to scream. He wanted to tell her that he couldn't be patient when Kassandra's life was on the line. He wanted to tell her that every moment they weren't finding her was a moment she was trapped, immobile in a cage underground.

He was so frustrated and he wanted to take it all out on her, the only God who'd believed him. One so nice and beautiful and kind. He caught himself just in time and walked away wordlessly. That was better than shouting at the God he liked best, who was his only ally right now. Trailing behind the class, Val left the forest and headed back to the castle.

Chapter 18

FEVER DREAMS

It was dark. Val could hear the dull buzzing of insects and the rustle of plants. He had a dull awareness of his body. It was limp and he was unable to move it. A quiet crunch synced up with the uncontrollable bobbing of his lolling head.

His eyes were open, he didn't know how he knew this, but he knew. It was pitch black, not even a glimmer of moonlight or stars could be seen. He felt a faraway hand on his lower back. He could tell it was there, steadying his floppy body. He surmised he was being carried again.

Was this the cloaked man?

Was this Loki?

Val's sluggish mind began racing. Had Loki got him too? It would make sense. Afterall he had been caught by the son of a Jotun twice now. Loki was a smart God, surely he knew what Val had been up to in his chambers that night. Had he simply been waiting for a good time to abduct him?

Val could smell the stagnant air of forest undergrowth. It was the scent of nature's decay, the death caused by the circle of life. Had he not been in the forest earlier that day for living off the land lessons he might not have realised. He was definitely in the forest. Of that, he was certain.

The crunch of footsteps continued, slowly, like a calm heartbeat. Val could hear the blood rushing to his head and he knew he was hanging upside down. He must be being carried over Loki's shoulder. At least he wasn't being dragged by the ankle.

It was cold, it reminded him of spring but of course it was summer now. Perhaps the forest gets cold at night even in summer, it's not like he would know. He hadn't left the castle at night since the beginning of the year when he skated on the icy lake with Kassandra.

Kassandra!

If he was being taken too, maybe he could save her? He could find a way out of the cages. This feeling was different to the dream he'd had after all. In the dream he couldn't even feel his body, but now he had an awareness of touch, even if it wasn't much. Maybe the spell or drug or whatever was causing the paralysis didn't work as well on him. This could be his ticket to saving her, and himself.

If she was even still in the cage.

A wave of sudden despair swarmed Val. What if she wasn't there. What if she'd been moved somewhere else and this was a staging area? What if she was dead? It would be just his luck to manage to escape only to find that she was no longer there and he was too late.

He pushed those thoughts away. She had to be there. She had to be alive. There was no other way.

The crunching steps moved onwards and Val wondered how he would end up in the cave. There were some mountains on the other side of the lake but they were miles away. Was he being taken there? If so, would he even be able to remain conscious all that time?

He could already feel himself fading. Would it be better to give into it and save his strength, or force himself awake and try to learn something about his location. If he did manage to escape he would need to know where he was so he could return to the castle. That being said, would Kassandra even be able to walk? If he had to carry her back from the mountain he'd definitely need all the strength he could muster – if he even had the strength to carry her that far in the first place.

His head hurt. So many thoughts all racing around the track in his mind. Was this a stress headache? He tried to concentrate on his breathing, a meditation technique his doctor had taught him to help with social anxiety when he was a kid.

In for two, out for four.

In for two, out for four.

Just like the doctor said. He started to calm down a little bit. Flooding his mind with a simple task helped him to quiet his thoughts.

It was quiet now, he could think more carefully and without intrusion from the negative voices. Always present, never shutting up and letting him think.

It was too quiet.

The crunching steps had stopped. He strained to see in the darkness but couldn't make anything out. His head started spinning again. Had he done the breathing technique wrong? He was feeling light headed. He fought to keep his eyes open but could feel their lids struggling.

There was a crash.

Val gasped for breath, his stomach contracted and forced him to sit upright. His body was soaking wet, it was cold. He looked around and realised he was in his bed. It was dark, lit only by the moonlight from outside. The curtainless window allowing the light to stream in. He turned to look towards it and saw a full circle of a moon. It was so big, taking up most of the window. It had a strange red glow.

Was this an omen? Was he dreaming? Maybe he was still being carried through the woods and had just passed out. It was hard to tell, both realities felt so real. He stood up, his legs numb and a little bit shaky. He looked around the room and saw three humps under blankets. The others were asleep.

He got dressed, a little wobbly. He walked towards the door and entered the common area. If this wasn't a dream then had the woods being another vision? If so, was he seeing through Kassandra's eyes again? If he was then she must have been moved from the cave. He couldn't risk it, he would have to venture into the woods and try to find her.

He moved towards the shield door, keeping his steps light as he had learnt in assassination class.

"Sneaking out again mate?" A voice he knew all too well said from the darkness.

"Why are you here?" Val asked coldly, stopping dead in his tracks and clenching his fists.

"You were moaning in your sleep. It woke me up so I thought I'd come wait here in case you decided to do something stupid again." The fire flickered to life and Val saw Alex sat back on his haunches beside it.

"You can't stop me." Val said icily, looking at the boy he once called friend.

"Wouldn't dream of it mate, but you're not going alone either." Alex smiled, getting to his feet.

"Why don't you tell us about your dream." Alice said moving out from the shadows and surprising Val.

Val hadn't even realised she was there. He hadn't spoken to either of them in weeks. He thought they hated him.

He had cast them aside. They were dead weight on his journey. They'd betrayed him, told him it wasn't Loki when he was so adamant that it was. But, despite all of that, despite the fire of burning rage to keep him warm, loneliness is always freezing.

All he had wanted these last few weeks was for them to believe him, to force him to talk to them. They had given up on him, or had he forced them away. Maybe this was his fault and not theirs. He had been consumed by anger and a worry for the girl he liked.

It was more than that. He felt responsible for her disappearance. It was his fault for letting her take the blame for his stupid skating idea. He felt ashamed and he had been taking it out on his friends. Yet there they were, acting as if nothing had happened.

For a split second, he felt warm. He moved towards the fire, hoping to dry off from the cold sweat and recanted his tale.

He told them how he wasn't sure if it even was Kassandra, how he believed it was him. How after waking he couldn't tell which reality was real. They listened silently.

"So she's being moved through the woods then?" Alice asked, leaning against the wooden wall.

"I think so." Val replied, taking a breath, head hanging.

Alice moved towards him and put her warm, soft hand on his arm. He realised he had been shaking, was it adrenaline, the cold, or something else? He didn't know, but her touch was the first he'd felt in a while and it was nice.

He felt tears welling up inside of him. The pain of being alone starting to lift. He'd pushed it down so deep, fallen into a silent rage for so long that he didn't even realise all of these emotions were in him.

"Well then let's go." Alex said, heading towards the shield door and looking back at him.

"Hold on a minute. Val, I've been thinking, trying to piece together the information we have and I wanted to ask you about that light you kept seeing." She said, looking directly into his glistening eyes.

Val had completely forgotten. He thought back to the beginning of term, when they had been taken by the Gods. He kept seeing a flicker of a light near the forest. Night after night. He hadn't seen it in months though. He told them as much and Alice let go of his arm. She moved towards the warm glowing fire, the flickering flames dancing on her scarlet hair.

"So, you haven't seen the light since students stopped going missing then?" She asked thoughtfully, twirling a strand of scarlet, ringleted hair.

Val thought back. Now she mentioned it, the light was always visible around the time the students were going missing. He hadn't noticed it before because people went missing all the time and he saw the light quite often. He hadn't seen the light since yule. That was nearly six months ago.

The he remembered!

He'd seen it, just for a second, right before he had his vision of Kassandra. He looked at Alice with eyes wide and told her. She paused for a moment, deep in thought.

"I think we should wait for the light then." Alice said, lowering her twiddling hand.

"But Kassandra is already in the woods, haven't we already missed it?" Val asked confused, pulling on the back of his hair.

Alex looked confused as well. Alice moved back towards them, grabbing both of their hands and holding them close to her chest. She looked earnestly at them both in turn.

"We can't just go stumbling around in the dark, I think this is our best shot at finding her." She said gazing deep into Val's eyes.

"Besides, we don't even know that what you saw was happening in the present. What if it was a vision of the past, of when she was first taken?"

Val thought back, the book had said that visions could sometimes be of the past or of a shared link. It didn't explicably say that they had to be happening at the moment you saw them.

Besides, Val trusted her. His doubts and feelings of betrayal were disappearing. He was so thankful to have his friends helping him again. He'd go with Alice's plan and pray that she was right. He agreed to her plan and she pulled both him and Alex into a tight warm hug.

"I've missed you." She said sincerely, her warm breath rasping on his neck.

He had missed her too. He'd missed them both. They took a moment to compose themselves whilst Alice wiped her eyes, then quietly left the common area and snuck through the familiar corridor and into the hall.

They left via the giant raven door and crept down towards the forest. Positioning themselves against the castle wall so they didn't cast a silhouette, Val's idea, they laid on the ground facing the forest. Making themselves as small as possible. His determination to learn from Loki might just be paying off now.

The three laid there for a while, silently. They stared relentlessly at the forest and Val willed the light to appear. Every moment they laid on the soft grass, Kassandra was being dragged further away. It was agonising. Val wanted nothing more than to go charging in but he knew Alice was right. They wouldn't find Kassandra by stumbling around blindly in the dark. He trusted her judgement, but it was still hard to wait there. He wasn't a patient person.

His legs were going numb with the night air, there was a whistling wind careening through the trees. It beckoned him to enter the forest.

Footsteps.

He heard crunching footsteps coming from behind him, to the right. He saw a stream of dim light as the raven doors opened. A shadowed figure stood still and listened for the patter of footfall before heading towards the forest. It was checking it wasn't being followed.

Val looked at Alex on his left and Alice on his right, they had heard it too. They stayed still, barely daring to breathe. The footsteps became quieter and a dim light flickered at the edge of the woods.

This was it.

Chapter 19

INTO THE WOODS

Alice stood up carefully and held out her hand to Val. He took it, needing the help off the ground as his numb legs weren't listening to him. Alex stood up as well and the three walked slowly towards the light.

Val's heart was racing. This was it. It must be Loki, Val had finally gotten the better of him. Now he could rescue Kassandra.

They walked slowly, taking deliberate steps and scanning the ground for twigs and branches. They wanted their steps to be as silent as possible. It was a kind of irony that the stalking skills Loki had taught them would be how they managed to follow him. A poetic irony that was not lost on Val.

They reached the edge of the forest and could vaguely see the dim light a few layers in. Val knew that light appeared closer than it really was in the darkness. It was also visible for miles under the right conditions – another snippet of knowledge Loki had taught him in assassination class.

Still being careful to limit their noise they followed the light.

Wet leaves and foliage caressed Val's trousers making them wetter than they already were. The whistling wind cut like a cold blade on the wet spots. It was uncomfortable and definitely not a pain he would have been able to handle before being subjected to the classes of Odinsall. The dim light bobbed and flickered as Loki weaved in and out of the trees.

Alice was breathing heavy next to Val. Her breath was loud and a little erratic. He reached for her hand and held it tight. Though he couldn't see her, he felt her eyes looking at him. Her breathing started to shallow and become more deliberate. He was glad.

Alex followed slightly behind. Stealth wasn't her strongest suit so he tried to copy Val's steps, not wanting to be the one who made the noise that would alert Loki to their presence.

They followed the dim light through the woods for a little while and soon they were on the edge of a clearing. It was the same clearing they had used for archery and living off the land lessons. They saw Freya's new hut and the light danced behind it. Val wondered if Freya was still inside, maybe it was worth checking and asking her for help. He decided against it, she was probably fast asleep in her cosy fur lined chambers back at the castle anyway. There wasn't time to check.

The trio slipped around the hut and followed the light off the beaten track into a built up wall of foliage and dense trees. They moved slower, walking almost at a crawl. It was difficult not to make any noise in here.

The light was getting further away from them. Obviously, Loki believed he was alone. He disappeared behind one of the many trees, but this time there was no flicker. The light didn't come back.

Val stopped and the others stopped behind him. Had they noticed that the light had gone? Had Loki realised he was being followed?

Val held his breath and listened hard. He could hear the dull buzz of insects. He heard the wind playfully tickling the tree leaves. He could not, however hear Loki.

He heard no steps, no brushing of leaves and foliage, no snapping twigs. Either Loki was standing still too, listening for them, or he had gone.

Alice pressed her lips against Val's ear and he fell victim to a cold, striking shiver. His neck hair stood on end and his entire body tingled.

"I think he's gone." She said barely moving her lips, allowing only the slightest sound to carry on her warm breath.

"We should keep going." Alex said from behind, still whispering but way too loudly.

If Loki didn't know they were there before, he certainly did now. Whispers carry on the wind in dark and quiet settings and can sometimes be more audible than normal talking from far away.

Val just had to hope that Loki wasn't stood still waiting for them. With a staggered sigh he began moving forwards, cats out of the bag now. He either knows they're here or he's already gone.

They reached the spot where Val thought he had last seen the light and there was no one there.

Where had he gone? Was he hiding about to jump out at them? Val was scared and he presumed the others were as well. Still he pressed on. He was sure the light had gone dark around here. He looked around, unable to see much in the dark, just the vague shadows and outlines of tall trees.

Hugging the trees, he started feeling around them for some sign that Loki had been there. A torn piece of clothing, a warm spot where the light had touched bark – if it was indeed a flame. Anything to let him know he was in the right place.

He looked around to see if his friends had found something. He reached out and found Alice.

"Any luck?" He whispered, lightly grasping her arm.

"No, Alex how about you?" She asked in hushed tones, looking behind her.

There was no reply.

Val's heart pounded. Had they being caught again? Where was Alex and was he ok? Val was scared, even the whistling wind jolted him as it passed through the trees.

"Alex, where are you?" He whispered, a little louder this time.

Alice held onto his hand, squeezing the blood from it and crushing his fingers. Val looked around and could just about make out a bit of trampled foliage. He stepped onto it, hoping that was where Alex had being last. He took another step forward and felt only air. For a fraction of a moment he felt weightless. Then gravity took hold.

He fell fast and hard into nothingness. Alice might have avoided the fall but she was gripping Val's hand so tightly he pulled her down with him. Together they dropped into the abyss. Val fell hard onto something soft and mere moments afterwards, Alice landed on top of him. For a small girl she really knocked the wind out of him. He gasped for breath, resisting the urge to cry out in pain.

A little dazed, he sat up, pushed Alice of him, and tried to get his bearings. He was obviously underground so maybe this was Loki's hide out. He looked around and saw dim lights coming from further in. A shadow moved and he realised it was a figure. His body tensed up involuntarily and he couldn't move. The shadow approached, holding it's right index finger to its lips menacingly. It stepped into the grey light coming through the hole.

It was just Alex.

Alex moved closer and using his index and forefinger, he pointed to his eyes and towards the dim light further in the tunnel. He must have been trying to tell them that something was in that direction.

Was it Loki?

Val wondered if Kassandra was there too. He looked over to Alice who was rubbing the back of her head. She was moving at least, so she was probably ok, after all he had cushioned her landing. He placed his hand on the floor to help guide himself up and felt something soft. It was a pile of furs, and he surmised that they were strategically placed for Loki's landings on his regular trips down the hole.

He stood up, feeling a dull pain in his tail bone. He was unsteady on his feet, but determined to walk it off and find Kassandra. Val offered out his hand to Alice who gladly took it. He hoisted her off of the floor and the two stepped towards Alex. Together they ventured towards the dim light.

It was dark and Val rubbed his hands along the walls to steady himself. They were jagged, raw earth. It reminded him of his vision from before. Was this the place? He walked slowly and deliberately towards the light. As they got closer he started to wonder if that light was Loki and if so, he must have heard their crash landing.

He decided it was too late to worry about that now and to just keep going. They reached the light and saw that it was a lit torch, bolted onto the bare earth wall. Val knew then that this was the place. It was the tunnel Kassandra was carried through in his dream.

They followed the tunnel for a while and Val got a distinct feeling he was heading downwards. Despite the flames from the torches, it was getting colder as they continued deeper in. After a while the tunnel got a little wider and they came across an annex of sorts. Inside were a few stacked cages.

The walls were fronted with wooden planks and thick wooden beams were strategically placed for structural stability.

Alice gasped and ran over to the closest cage on the right. She bent down and appeared to be looking at something. Val moved closer and looked over her shoulder.

He saw a skeleton like boy with brunette hair. He was crammed inside the cage and Val couldn't tell if he was even alive.

"It's Tom." Alice whimpered, pulling on Val's cloak.

She was right. Val leant closer and Tom's eyes moved to meet his. Only his eyes moved. It was creepy, like a reanimated corpse. Tom looked like he hadn't eaten in weeks. His cheeks were sallow and his skin had turned a pale grey. Val could clearly see his rib cage through a half rotted green polo. He was a gruesome and sorry sight.

He looked towards Alice and saw her covering her mouth, he eyes were welling up. It was a lot to take in.

Alex came towards them from further in.

"There's a person in every cage. I think they're the missing students." He whispered when he got close enough.

Val moved away from Tom and began looking around and Alex was right.

"There must be a key somewhere." Val whispered as he felt the walls and moved around the annex.

However, he had no luck. He went back to Tom's cage and tried to force open the door. It was no use, the iron bars were welded tight and he simply wasn't strong enough.

"We can't leave him." Alice cried, tears now caressing her soft red cheeks.

"I know, but we need to keep moving. We can't get him out unless we find the key and I bet Loki has it." Val said, taking her hand to help her off of her knees.

He gave her a soft hug and lead her away.

Val looked back and saw Tom staring at him with pleading eyes. He felt rotten, leaving his friend like that but he knew it was the only way to help him.

He would have to defeat Loki.

Chapter 20

THE CAVE

Val lead the others further through the tunnels with gritted teeth. He knew what awaited him. The question was: how can a normal person defeat a God?

As they continued deeper in the air around them got colder. With only the dim light of the wall mounted torches to guide them to their destination. Along the way they came across other small annex rooms, each stacked with cages, only some of the cages had occupants but they all looked as bad as Tom did.

How many was he planning to abduct? Was there a cage for all of the students?

Interestingly, Val didn't know who all of the captives were. There were only one hundred and fifty humans at Odinsall and though some had gone missing, he didn't remember it being this many.

After walking through what felt like miles of tunnels and a handful of annex's they arrived at a small door.

"This is it." Val whispered to his two friends.

He opened the door slowly and entered. They were in a much larger room this time, it seemed familiar. There were cages lining the walls but they were mostly empty. They walked towards the centre of the room but there was no sign of Loki.

Then Val realised.

This was the room from his vision of Kassandra and that must mean her shackled cage was in here.

Almost forgetting the danger he was in, Val turned and ran to the right hand side of the room, near the opposite end from the door. That's where she was in his dream. It was only a short sprint as the room wasn't that big. He reached the spot and dropped to his knees.

There she was, shackled to the back of a larger cage. Her body was limp and her head lolled onto her chest. She was a sorry sight. She had definitely lost weight but she wasn't a skeleton just yet, not like Tom had being. Still, Val started welling up, he couldn't help it.

"Kassandra." He said just louder than a whisper, tears filling his eyes.

"I'm here, I'm going to save you."

Her eyelids flickered ever so slightly, but they did not open. He was relieved, he took that as a sign that she was alive and right now that was all that mattered. He reached through the cage's iron bar and was just able to brush the edge of her thigh. He was trying to be comforting but he couldn't quite reach far enough for it to take full effect, or so he thought.

"I think this is the last room." Alice whispered, standing somewhere behind him.

Val turned around and saw she was stood next to a door. There was a shimmering blue light coming through the cracks.

Val stood up.

"I'll be back for you. I promise." He said determinedly, looking back at Kassandra.

He walked towards Alice, fists clenched. He reached for the door handle and together the three of them entered.

The room was awash with a dazzling blue glow coming from the ceiling. It was an oval shaped room, sparsely decorated. The ceiling itself looked like water. It was mesmerising, it might have been beautiful under different circumstances. Loki stood in the middle of the room with his back to them and his hood up.

Val approached him and stopped just a few feet away. His fists still clenched, he was ready.

"Let them go." He commanded in a voice he barely recognised as his own.

"You took your time getting here." Said the hooded figure.

Val took a step back, he looked at Alex who looked back at him sharing the same puzzled look. This can't be Loki, it's not his voice. But it had to be Loki, they only found the place by following him. He was the son of a Jotun, he was mean and everything about his character fit the bill.

"Surprised?" The hooded figure said as it turned to face him.

Slowly the figure pulled down their hood and smiled a sinister smile at Val.

It was Freya.

Val was shocked beyond belief. Freya had always been so nice to him. She was the only one who believed him when he had the visions. She was kind and sweet and beautiful. Most of all she wasn't Loki, the man he had grown to despise.

"It's you." He said, unable to get anything else out.

"That's right and it must be so shocking for you." She laughed.

"Beautiful, harmless Freya. But how? I thought Loki was the evil one?" She said in a mimicking tone.

Val took another step back. This was Freya, but her personality had completely changed. The kind, warm God he knew was acting cynical and mean. Her face was contorted and her smile curved mostly on one side. A grinning, taunting, grotesque smile. Her delicate features and beautiful face definitely didn't match the look in her eyes.

"But how, I followed Loki down here." Val said in disbelief, mouth agape.

"You followed me you stupid boy." She shouted, slicing her arm through the air.

"You've been following exactly what I wanted you to follow since the very beginning. My plan was going perfectly until you and your little friends decided to sneak out and speak to All Father. He's been hot on my tail ever since. I had to switch tactics after that." She said erratically, gritting her teeth as she spat the words at them.

"How do you think you got those visions. What, did you think you were special or something?" She sneered meanly.

Val's head was spinning. She'd been playing him this whole time? How can that be? He was so confused, he was so certain it would be Loki under that hood.

"Poor Kassandra. You don't deserve her, she's clever. Clever enough to have seen through my acting. That's why I had to bring her down here, she was collateral damage. Ah, but then, then I realised I could use her to get to you. Val Jones, the insignificant child of Loki, always surrounded by at least two other brats. Three more prisoners for my collection for the price of one." She laughed manically, clutching her stomach.

"B-but why?" Alice shouted from next to Val.

"Why are you kidnapping people?"

Alice's lip was quivering and her hands were shaking. She copied Val and clenched her fists, determined to be brave. She had looked up to Freya as a powerful and beautiful role model. Living proof that a woman could have it all in this world.

"Why? I thought you'd have figured that out sweet Alice. You're the smart one aren't you? Obviously not smart enough. I guess I can tell you, it's not like it matters much now anyway. It's for the Neo Jotun Army! All Father and his band of merry idiots hunted the Jotun almost to extinction and it is my goal to bring them back." She smirked, clearly loving the power she currently held over them.

"Why does it have to be humans?" Alex asked quietly.

"We never did anything to you, we didn't even ask to be brought here." He said, visibly shaking.

Val, looked at Alex for a second and could see a popping vein on his forehead. He looked furious. Val had never seen him like this before.

"Because humans have more mouldable blood and they're easier to steal. You humans are powerless against a God like me. You three in particular will make good specimens, just like that other boy. You see, it turns out the blood you share with Loki makes it easier to transform you. He's half Jotun after all." Freya snarked, pacing menacingly in front of them.

Val's head was spinning. It didn't make any sense. He felt dizzy and a little sick. He looked to his friends who seemed to be feeling the same. He took a deep breath. It might not be Loki but he still had to stop this. He needed to save Kassandra. That was all that mattered. He willed his body to move and lunged at Freya.

If he could just get the key and get back through the door. Maybe that would be enough. He didn't really have a plan, he didn't even know where the key to the cages was. Did it even have a key? There was no time to think about that now. His legs exploded. With all the power he could muster he lunged.

He neared Freya who hadn't yet reacted. He was hoping to take her by surprise. Then, with lightning speed she flicked her arm at him and swatted him like a fly. Val flew through the air to the side of Freya and hit the wall hard. His body crumpled to the floor and he couldn't breathe. His lungs were emptied of all their air.

"Stupid boy." She said quietly, blowing on her knuckles.

She advanced towards Alex and swiftly punched him in the stomach before he could react. He fell to his knees, blood dripping out of his mouth. Alice screamed and ran towards Val who was struggling to get to his feet. Like a bolt of lightning Freya was upon them. She grabbed Alice by the throat one handed and lifted her off the ground. Alice clawed at her hands and kicked out but it was no use. Freya was too powerful, her strength was otherworldly.

Time stood still. Val watched Alice struggle against Freya's unnatural grip-strength. He saw Alex, unmoving, blood mid drip from his open mouth. He was powerless to help them. It was hopeless. What could he, a painfully average human boy, do against a God?

He wished he could help them. He wished he had the power to save his friends.

"It seems the spirit of battle has awakened within you." Hissed a familiar voice.

"I can give you power. The power to save your friends. A power known only in this realm."

Val realised it was the same voice he heard when he touched the blood stone all those months ago. The hissing serpentine voice from inside him.

"Who are you?" Val asked, though unbeknownst to him, his lips were not moving.

"Why I am you, the other you. The you who knows your deepest desires." It hissed.

"Just say yes and I will grant you power."

Val didn't have time to think. He wanted, no, he needed to save his friends. It was his fault they were here in the first place. Throwing caution to the wind, he greedily accepted the offer.

The room was back in motion. Alice was kicking out against Freya who had her by the throat. Alex was bleeding from the mouth, kneeling on the floor. Val didn't feel any different. He was still struggling to breathe and his chest was in agony. He put his hand out trying to stand up and felt something there. Looking down he saw a silver hilted dagger. There was no mistaking it, this was the dagger he had seen in Loki's draw.

He lifted it up and looked at it. Was this his power? It was only a dagger.

"Become the unnoticed." The hissing voice said in the back of Val's mind.

He had no idea what that meant. That being said, if he could catch Freya off guard she might release Alice just long enough for them to escape. He got to his feet, clutching his burning, aching chest with one hand, dagger held by his side with the other. Steadily he walked towards Freya, he lifted the dagger and plunged it into her side.

How hadn't she seen him? She reacted so fast before.

Freya let out a blood curdling scream. It was a monstrous sound, not even human – or Godly. She dropped Alice who crumpled to the floor gasping for breath. He slid the dagger out, as if pulling it from a sheath. He pulled his arm back ready to strike again.

Before he could, Freya turned to him. Her beautiful face was now twisted, turning a pale blue, as if she was something else entirely. She glared at him through the pain. Her eyes burned with a searing hatred.

Then she vanished.

Val looked at the spot where she had just been in disbelief. Where had she gone. Surely a little stab wound wasn't enough to kill her. There was a clatter and a small, golden key dropped to the floor right where she had being standing.

Had they won?

Alex stumbled to his feet and with both hands clutching at his stomach, he walked towards Alice.

"Where's Val?" He asked, doubled over.

Alice looked around, seemingly staring straight through Val.

"I don't know, she didn't take him did she?" Alice said worriedly, moving her head as if she was searching for him.

Val was confused. He was stood right there, he was literally less than a meter from Alice.

"I'm literally right here guys." He said, slightly annoyed. This was not a good time for weird jokes.

They both jumped and looked at him startled.

"How did you do that?" Alex asked in awe, now looking at him rather than through him.

"How did I do what?" Val said. This joke was getting out of hand and he was getting more annoyed at his friends by the second.

"I can explain it." Said a warm, kind of familiar voice, from across the room.

All three of them turned at once. At the other side of the room was what looked like a jail cell. Val walked towards it, slowly and in pain. Sitting calmly on a small wooden bench was Freya.

"I knew it wouldn't be that easy." Val said raising his dagger. Too tired and in pain to be shocked anymore.

"Hold your horses kiddo, I'm no threat to you." Freya said playfully stroking her long blonde hair.

Val was conflicted. There in front of him sat the evil woman he had just stabbed. However, there was no blood or stab wound and her personality had done a U-turn. Oddly, it was a slightly different personality to the Freya he had liked before entering the cave.

"That monster you just fought wasn't me. I've been stuck in this hole for nearly a year." Freya said, getting to her feet and approaching the iron bars.

She went on to explain that almost a year ago, just before the students were brought to Odinsall, she was captured. Freya had been hunting in these very woods when a huge white stag ran across her path. She gave chase, hoping to catch it, but the stag rushed her, antlers first, and knocked her unconscious and she woke up in this cell.

"I later discovered that the stag was actually a Jotun called Ymir and he had the power to transform into other people and animals." She finished, looking each of them up and down in turn.

Val took a step back. Her story, as outlandish as it seemed, did make sense for this realm. After all, he'd seen Loki transform from a cat only a few weeks ago. If this was true though, then how could he know that Loki wasn't really the Jotun all along?

"I think she's telling the truth." Alice said, echoing the thought's Val had just had.

"Yeah me too, I'll go grab the key." Val replied, turning painfully on the spot.

Chapter 21

FIRST LOVE

Val limped back to the middle of the shimmering blue room. Clutching his chest, the pain getting worse, he knelt down and picked up the small, golden key. He stumbled back towards Freya's cell. Trembling, probably from the left over adrenaline, he opened the large, iron barred door.

Freya got to her feet and stepped out into the room. The sparkling blue light danced across her porcelain skin, highlighting her gorgeous, symmetrical face. She had soft looking cheeks and large eyes. The fake Freya paled in comparison. A perfect imitation yes, but missing something. Just what that something was, Val couldn't quite tell.

"Ok I freed you, now please will you help me with the kidnap victims?" Val wheezed, doubling over as he struggled to breathe.

His chest felt as if it was caved in and speech and breathing were becoming harder by the minute. Despite that, he had to free Kassandra. Freya agreed to help. She had Val put his arm around her and she helped him walk back towards Kassandra's cage. Her shoulders were sturdy, yet soft and pleasant to the touch. He could tell she was athletically powerful and it reassured him to have her with them.

Alice and Alex hobbled together behind them, holding each other for support. They looked worse for wear. Val regretted dragging them with him, though he couldn't have found the cave by himself. He was a bad friend, always putting his wants and needs above theirs. In a way, Val had never really seen the realm of the Gods as a real place. He realised he'd been living as if it was all a dream. Only now did he see how reckless and selfish that thought was. As he looked back at his injured friends, he felt a rain of sadness falling over him.

"Do you know what the blue light is Freya?" Alice asked curiously, her voice barely a hoarse whisper.

"I think it's the lake darling." She said, as she helped Val to walk.

This new Freya was odd. She didn't speak like the other Gods, she spoke more like a human from their realm. Val thought back to the books he'd seen on the human realm in All Father's office all those months ago. Maybe Freya had read them as well? Regardless, the fact that she talked in a familiar way made her easier to like.

With Freya's help, Val made it back through the door and over to Kassandra's cage. Her eyes were still closed and her wrists shackled to the far side of the iron prison. He dropped to his knees, because he didn't have the strength to lower himself down.

Shakily he placed the small, golden key into the lock and heard a click. The iron bars slowly creaked open and Val crawled inside towards Kassandra. He undid her shackles and one by one her wrists flopped to her side. She was almost lifeless.

Mustering the little strength he had left he cradled her limp body in his arms and struggled to pull her out of the cage. Her eyelids twitched and he couldn't tell if she was conscious, but he was certain that she was alive.

"It's ok, I'm going to get you out of here." He whispered shakily.

His eyes glistened over. Seeing her like that, almost lifeless. It was an awful sight, especially for a boy of only sixteen. A single tear fell from his eye and landed on her forehead. It trickled downwards, falling off of her chin and disappearing down her chest.

"Come on, we need to get back to Odinsall. We can't carry them all out at once and you kids need to heal." Freya said commandingly, gesturing towards the door they had just come through.

Val struggled to his feet and Freya helped him walk again, taking most of Kasandra's weight herself.

"How do we get out?" Alice asked, her head under Alex's arm, helping to take some of his weight.

"We fell down a hole to get here."

She raised a good point. Unless Freya could fly, they were trapped down in the dim, cold cave.

"Don't worry, I've seen Ymir leave countless times and he never turned into a bird." Freya smiled, trying to lighten the situation.

Freya lead them back into the blue room. She positioned them all in the centre of the room, where her doppelganger had disappeared from only minutes ago.

"Look at the floor." She said.

Val hadn't noticed before but there was a large circle of runes on the floor. In the middle of the runes was a huge vegvisir, just like the one on the pendant Alice had given him at yule. That felt like a lifetime ago now. The vegvisir was the Norse rune of safe travelling.

"You all need to hold hands, otherwise my seidr won't spread to you." She instructed, grasping Val's hand whilst holding Kassandra with her other, outstretched arm.

They complied, standing in a circle like they were about to perform a pagan ritual. Freya spoke a weird phrase in a language Val couldn't understand. There was a flash of blue light and suddenly they were standing on the dock.

Val felt a gust of fresh air tussle his hair. He looked around and could see the large moon emitting it's strange red glow across the lake. The calm water twinkled like a mirror or a portal, reflecting the shimmering stars above. It was almost serene.

Freya lead them, injured and limping back towards the castle. Trying to lighten the mood she made some small talk along the way. This was strange for a God, none of the others really seemed to do that.

"So, what did imposter me teach you?" She asked, looking at them from in front.

"The art of seduction." Alex replied through difficult breaths.

"The art of seduction? What on Midgard is that?" She scoffed, clearly insulted.

"I'm a God of hunting, not flirting!" She said indignantly, flipping her hair with a swift head flick.

Val chuckled but it hurt his chest even more. He didn't mind though, it was nice to feel a little happiness after all they'd just been through.

As they approached the castle Val could have sworn he saw the left raven's eye move to look at them. The doors swung open without them having touched them. All Father was stood there, his one eye looking at them all in turn.

"Go get the healer." All Father commanded, looking at the raven doors with his one eye. From behand him Huginn flew out of the secret passage and shot through the hall.

"Freya, what has happened?" All Father asked, sounding concerned and moving towards them.

Freya filled him in, explaining firstly about the children in the cages. As she did All Father began sending commands to his staff of Gods and pretty soon most of the castle was awake and helping out in one way or another. Val wanted to talk to him, he had so many questions, but now was not the time.

The healer barged through the door at the back left of the hall and ran towards them.

"Oh my, look at the state of you. Come with me, come now." She said motherly, grabbing Val's hand and starting to drag him away.

Val looked back at Freya who smiled at him and pushed him gently with one hand. With Alice's help, he carried Kassandra behind the healer as she led them to her chambers. She held the door open ushering them inside.

"Lay her down there." She said pointing towards a fur covered bed in the corner.

Alex and Val stumbled towards the bed and gently laid Kassandra down. Her limp hand fell off the side of the bed, dangling in mid-air. He'd made it. Val had saved her. He felt a sudden wave of fatigue rush over him and he started to go light headed. He stumbled back, and his hand lost its strength sending the silver hilted dagger sprawling across the floor.

"Where did you get this?" The healer said picking the dagger up off of the floor.

"I guess that doesn't matter now." She pondered, placing the dagger on a bedside table.

She moved towards Val and lightly pushed him onto a bed behind him. She smiled at him and turned to Alex and Alice, urging them to do the same. The two sat down on other beds and Alex doubled over, vomiting more blood.

"What on earth has happened to you poor kids." The healer said, hands on her hips and concerned.

She moved towards Kassandra and put her ear to her chest. She then did the same to her mouth and felt her forehead with the back of her hand.

"This is dark seidr. I'll need to make an herbal medicine to bring her around." She said solemnly.

"You can wake her up though right?" Val asked, clutching his chest.

"I can but not without the right ingredients. Right now I think you three need to be checked over." She said, moving towards Val.

Val protested, he didn't care about his own injuries. Val and the healer came to a compromise in that she would see to Alex and Alice first, but in return Val would have to lay down and try to steady his breathing. He did this but each breath was a striking stab wound to the chest. He was wheezing and his lungs burned, fighting for oxygen.

The healer treated Alex first. He had internal bleeding and she surmised that some of his internal organs were badly bruised – explaining the blood coming from his mouth. She moved away from Alex and opened a tall, oak cabinet. Inside there were weird looking plants and glasses, corked bottles with crushed up herbs.

She took a few bottles down from the cabinet and meticulously measured out various powders and plant leaves. She added these ingredients into a mortar and used a pestle to press them together. She made quick work of the odd task and then emptied the resulting powder into a small tankard. She stirred this and then returned to Alex, holding it to his lips.

"You need to drink every drop. It's mixed with honey mead so it shouldn't taste too bad." She smiled sadly.

Alex dutifully guzzled the mixture. By the time he had drank the last drop his head started to loll. The healer caught him, gently placing her hand on the back of his neck. She lowered him down onto the pillow, as he unconsciously wheezed. She then hoisted off his bloodied, green polo and looked at his stomach. It was a dark shade of purple. She murmured to herself and went back to the cabinet, pulling out a large tub of salve. She rubbed this into the bruising and bandaged the area with a strange, leather-like material.

She then moved onto Alice who's injury was on her neck. She had deep black finger marks where Ymir had strangled her.

"I'm surprised you can talk with bruises this deep." The healer said, holding Alice's chin and moving her head gently, side to side.

Alice tried to answer but only a high pitched whistling croak escaped her swollen lips.

"Ah, it seems you managed on adrenaline alone. Don't worry dear, we'll have that lovely voice back in no time." The healer smiled.

She gently rubbed the salve on Alice's neck and wrapped it in the same, odd leather-like bandage. She then returned to her cabinet and table and mixed up a solution using different herbs and leaves. She helped Alice to drink it and, like Alex, her head lolled and soon she was sleeping on the healer's bed.

"Now it's your turn youngling." She said walking towards Val.

She helped him take off his ripped, dusty polo and began running her hand over his chest. Val winced with the pain, but tried not to show it.

"You have a few broken ribs. You're lucky, if they had snapped any further they might have pierced your lung entirely." She mused.

As with the others, the healer applied the salve to Val's injury. It was warm and penetrated deep into his skin. The feeling was pleasant, though a little sticky. She wrapped his chest with the same weird bandage. She then created another mixture and asked Val to drink it. It tasted a bit like honey mead but it was bitter and bitty. It wasn't very kind on the throat either. He battled through the pain of swallowing and his eyes became heavy. His entire body was weighted and he too, fell into a deep sleep.

By the time Val had woken the healer's chamber was full with wall to wall beds. They must have made or brought more in as the captured students were recovered. Val sat up, his head groggy and looked around. He counted twenty one patients all in all, including Alex, Alice and Kassandra. He slipped out of bed and tried to get to his feet, but fell backwards onto the edge. The pain in his chest was now a dull ache, breathing still hurt but it was manageable.

"Morning mate." Alex said from across the room, sat up against the headboard of the bed.

"How you feeling?" Val asked, still holding his chest.

"Like I've been hit by a truck." He laughed with difficulty. "

You?"

"Yeah same." Val replied, chuckling himself.

He looked across at Kassandra who was now under the covers with a strange tube stuck in her left wrist. The tube was attached to a wooden pole and at the top was a covered tankard. The contraption resembled a drip from the hospitals back home but without the sanitary appearance.

Val looked to the other side of the room and saw Alice. She was laid on her side watching him. She lifted her hand slightly in a waving motion.

"Her voice is still sore, the healer reckons it'll be a few days before she can speak properly again." Alex explained.

Val looked at them both with sad eyes. They were beaten, bruised and lucky to be alive and it was his fault. He never should have lead them into danger.

"I know what you're thinking mate. Thing is, we made our own choices and we're all alive. So don't go beating yourself up eh?" Alex grinned.

Val looked at each of the other students in turn. They were all attached to the Nordic drips and they were all unmoving. Some were worse than others though. His eyes found Tom, who was by far the worst off. His ribs were showing like a rotten corpse. His upper arms were thinner than Val's forearms - and he was a beanpole by all accounts.

The poor boy must have been through hell. Whilst they celebrated yule and played raid battles he was rotting in a cage, all alone. Val couldn't even imagine the suffering he must have gone through.

The door opened and the healer walked in.

"Ah Val you're awake. How are you feeling?" She asked, stepping lightly towards him.

"Awful, but a lot better than I was. Thank you." He said, still clutching his chest.

She looked him up and down, seeing that he was half off the bed. She shook her head slightly, obviously not impressed.

"If you can walk, All Father would like a word with you. He's in the room next door." She said coldly as she moved away from Val to look at one of the kidnap victims.

Val stood, using the edge of the bed for support. He felt light headed but he'd never been one to stay in bed all day. Gingerly he walked towards the healer and with a last look at his friends and Kassandra, he left the room.

He staggered to the room next door and opened the small, oval door. All Father was stood at the back of the room, perusing a large tome. He turned around and smiled.

"Ah, young Val. Please sit down, we have much to discuss." He said warmly, looking at a chair.

Val took the closest seat to the door. It was a soft, leather armchair, not unlike the ones in Loki clan's common area. All Father placed the heavy tome down on a table and pulled up a stool that was sitting in the corner.

The room was warm and Val could smell a faint mint. He glanced around and saw multiple oak cabinets with ingredients inside. There were also baskets full of strange plants littering the floor. He wondered if this was the healers storeroom.

"How did you acquire this?" All Father asked curiously as he pulled the silver hilted dagger from somewhere inside his flowing cloak.

Val's memory was bit hazy. He was struggling to come to terms with exactly how he did receive the dagger. He recanted his tale the best he could and mentioned the hissing voice in his head that he'd heard once before. He also mentioned that the same voice spoke to him when he touched the blood stone.

Whilst Val told his story All Father sat and listened attentively. He sat forward with his hands tucked under his chin, like a child being told a bedtime story by its mother. When Val finally finished All Father sat up straight, crossed his right leg over his left and placed his clasped hands on his lap.

"It sounds like Jormungandr spoke to you." All Father said thoughtfully.

"What's a Jormungandr?" Val asked confused.

"He is the world serpent who connects the nine realms. It's exceedingly rare for him to talk to someone. He almost never communicates with us Gods." All Father explained, gesticulating lighty with his hands still mostly clasped together.

Val sat back, taking the pressure off of his broken ribs.

"Why would he give me the dagger?" Val asked, still confused.

"Ah, he must have recognised you as someone who could draw out its power. That dagger is called the blade of the unseen, it's an assassins weapon. If a person's soul resonates properly with the dagger they can almost become a shadow at will." All Father said, his eyes glinting in the light of the candles.

Val thought back to when he stabbed Freya. He did think it was odd that she didn't see him coming and block him like she had when he tried to attack her the first time. Then later on Alex and Alice said they couldn't see him. He thought it was a strange, poorly timed joke, but maybe they were being serious.

"When the blade connects with a user it allows them to blend in. It's not that they go invisible as such, just that other people don't really notice they're there – unless they're really looking for them or the user breaks the seidr." All Father said, as if reading Val's mind.

Val looked at the blade of the unseen which lay in All Father's lap. It was an ornate and cool looking weapon. Val was rather drawn to the oddly curved edge of the dagger. Was it really so special as to grant him that kind of power though?

"Sir, I first saw the dagger in Loki's chamber. Why did he have it?" Val asked, thinking back to when he had first seen it in the draw.

"How very astute of you young Val. Loki found the blade many moons ago, he knew what it was but he couldn't use it himself. Perhaps he brought it to Odinsall in the hopes of passing it along? You'd have to ask him yourself if you really want to know though." He smiled, knowingly.

The idea of asking Loki anything made Val's stomach churn. He might not have been behind the kidnappings but Val still hated him. There was no chance Loki would ever do anything as kind as brining a magical blade to help another person. He was way too self-serving for that.

"Anyhow, it's good that you bring up Loki. I want you to take special lessons with him next term. His powers are somewhat similar to that of the blade and I think he can help you learn to control it." All Father said slyly.

"Bu-" Val started to protest.

"I won't hear anything more on the matter. It is decided. Be thankful I'm letting you keep such a precious and sought after weapon young Val." All Father said sternly, waggling his finger at him like a dad lecturing a naughty child.

Val crossed his arms in silent protest. He didn't want anything to do with the trickster God. It was bad enough being in his house, let alone having to spend private time with him outside of regular classes.

"Is there anything more you want to ask me?" All Father asked, returning to his calm and kind demeanour.

Val thought for a moment. There were a whole host of questions but it seemed like All Father wanted him to leave. If he could only ask one question he'd better make it count.

"Who's Ymir and why could he give me visions?" Val asked suddenly.

"Ymir was the Jotun king. Many hundreds of years ago he raised an army of frost giants in the realm of Jotunheim and laid siege to the realm of the Gods. Many lost their lives in that battle, including my own son: Baldr. After years of bloody warfare we wiped out the entire Jotun race – or at least I thought we had, until today. There's small comfort in the plans Ymir told you. If he was trying to create more Jotun then that must mean he's the last, or one of the last, of his kind. That being said, even one Jotun is one too many." He said sadly, lowering his head.

Val wondered if Loki knew about this Ymir. He was half Jotun after all. Though, he didn't seemed to be involved with this kidnap plan so Val pushed the thought aside.

"As to why he can send you visions, I don't know. I think that maybe it only worked because he had captured Kassandra. You have strong feelings for her don't you." He said teasingly, his one eye trained on Val.

Val felt a hot flush come over his face and All Father laughed, just a little. All Father told Val that that was enough conversation for one day and he told him to return to the healer's chamber to rest.

After a few days of rest Val and his friends were allowed to return to the comfort of their own beds. The kidnapped students still hadn't recovered, but the healer promised to let them know as soon as someone woke up.

Dean and Simon apologised to Val for treating him like an outcast the past few weeks. Simon was especially thankful that he'd saved Tom. They told him that classes had been cancelled for the next month so the Gods could concentrate on healing the rescued students and give them all time to heal. Alex was especially thankful for this news, hating studying as he did.

The cancellation of classes also came with an even better reward: no exams. A reward that seemed more like a punishment to poor Alice who had pretty much recovered the use of her voice now and was using it to vocalise her disappointment. After all, she had studied more than anyone else and spent a lot of her free time in the archive.

The other members of Loki clan took every opportunity to talk to the exhausted trio. All Father wanted the event to remain secret, so naturally, the whole school knew. Even the other class one girls got involved, trying to tease extra details out of Alice, a girl who they had mostly ignored all year. It was a strange and, mostly joyous time.

Amidst the welcoming banter and new found respect from his peers, Odinsall was finally starting to feel like a home for Val. When he thought back over the year: the difficult classes, his inability to stand out for anything other than losing glory, the disappearing students and most painfully, the death of his mother and nearly all of his friends, he realised just how much he had changed.

He was no longer the socially anxious, average teenager. Well, mostly. He'd made friends, the likes of which he never really had back in his own world. The realm of the Gods was far from peaceful, it definitely wasn't an easy life, but somehow he'd pretty much made it through a year in this place.

A few days later one of the older boys came to the clan with news. The glory competition had been cancelled and would start from scratch next year. For the last place Loki clan, this was amazing news. Val smiled as he thought of Erik who must have been smashing chairs and punching walls in frustration.

Later that day whilst Val was eating dinner with his friends and clan, the healer came over. She told Val that Kassandra was now awake, the first one to do so in fact. This made sense as she was the one who was most recently kidnapped, so she wouldn't have been under the effects of the paralysis for too long. Val stood up, heart pounding and sprinted out of the hall without a word to anyone.

He raced through the corridor and crashed through the door to the healer's chamber. A little out of breath and sweating he stood still. His eyes were glued. There she was, they'd been through so much together but Val didn't even know if she remembered any of it. For all he knew she wasn't even conscious through it all. He walked towards the bedside where she sat up, looking worse for wear and staring back at   him.

He stood next to her bed. His heart was throbbing, something caught in his throat and he didn't know what to say. There was so much he wanted to tell her but at finally seeing her awake it was all he could do just to hold back the tears.

He was so emotional all of a sudden. He looked at her soft, delicate face. It was gaunter than he remembered. She was wearing a dark red vest with one shoulder hanging down. He gulped, aware of the sweat glistening on his brow.

"Kassandra I-"

Before he could finish she grabbed the collar of his polo shirt and pulled him into a heavy kiss. It was the only way she could truly convey her gratitude and affection for the boy who had saved her life.

What did you think of ODINSALL:

The Stolen Children?

First of all, thank you for purchasing this book. I know you could have picked any number of books to read but you picked this one and for that I am extremely grateful!

I hope the book provided a welcome escape from everyday life and that you enjoyed it. If so, it would be really nice if you could share this book with your friends and family by posting to ***Facebook***, ***Instagram*** and ***Twitter.***

If you enjoyed this book I would love to hear from you and hope that you could take the time to post a review on ***Amazon.*** Your feedback and support will help this author to greatly improve his writing craft for future projects and make this book even better!

I want you as the reader to know that your review and opinion is really important to me.

Once again, thank you so much for reading ODINSALL: *The Stolen Children.*

About the author:

Cullen Spurr is a writer and author of the ODINSALL Saga but he's also been a police officer, a guitarist in a metal band, a corporate content creator and, of course, an owner of a big, dopey mastiff / staffy dog. Cullen loves to create story driven fantasy novels, steeped in mythology and plot twists. He lives with his fiancé in Leeds, UK and has a BA Hons in English and Journalism and was the winner of the English and Journalism programme prize for academic achievement.

Acknowledgements:

I would like to say a special thanks to the following for supporting and always believing in me:

Leah Hall

Sharon Spurr

David Spurr

Logan Spurr

Daz Hall

Tracy Hall

Printed in Great Britain
by Amazon